HOME COMPUTERS

Books by Scott Corbett

The Trick Books

The Lemonade Trick
The Mailbox Trick
The Disappearing Dog Trick
The Limerick Trick
The Baseball Trick
The Turnabout Trick
The Hairy Horror Trick
The Home Run Trick
The Hockey Trick
The Black Mask Trick
The Hangman's Ghost Trick

Suspense Stories

Cop's Kid
Tree House Island
Dead Man's Light
Cutlass Island
One by Sea
The Baseball Bargain
Run for the Money
The Case of the Gone Goose
The Case of the Fugitive Firebug
The Case of the Ticklish Tooth
The Case of the Silver Skull
The Case of the Burgled Blessing Box

What Makes It Work?

What Makes a Car Go?
What Makes TV Work?
What Makes a Plane Fly?
What Makes a Boat Float?

Ghost Stories

The Red Room Riddle
Here Lies the Body
Captain Butcher's Body

Easy-to-Read Adventures

Dr. Merlin's Magic Shop
The Great Custard Pie Panic
The Boy Who Walked on Air
The Great McGoniggle's Gray Ghost
The Great McGoniggle's Key Play
The Great McGoniggle Rides Shotgun
The Foolish Dinosaur Fiasco
The Mysterious Zetabet

Nonfiction for Older Readers

Home Computers

HOME COMPUTERS

A SIMPLE AND
INFORMATIVE GUIDE

by Scott Corbett

An Atlantic Monthly Press Book

Little, Brown and Company
Boston   Toronto

COPYRIGHT © 1980 BY SCOTT CORBETT

FIRST EDITION

Library of Congress Cataloging in Publication Data

Corbett, Scott.
  Home computers.

  "An Atlantic Monthly Press book."
  Includes index.
  SUMMARY: An introduction to a variety of small computers and their uses in the home.
  1. Minicomputers — Juvenile literature.
  2. Microcomputers — Juvenile literature. [1. Mini-computers. 2. Microcomputers. 3. Computers]
  I. Title.
  QA76.5.C65   001.64′04   80–10636
  ISBN 0–316–15658–2

ATLANTIC–LITTLE, BROWN BOOKS
ARE PUBLISHED BY
LITTLE, BROWN AND COMPANY
IN ASSOCIATION WITH
THE ATLANTIC MONTHLY PRESS

BP

Published simultaneously in Canada
by Little, Brown & Company (Canada) Limited

PRINTED IN THE UNITED STATES OF AMERICA

To my nieces
Mary Ann and Suzanne,
both of whom
know more about computers
than I do

Preface

The only way to learn the simple facts about home computers, I decided, was to live with one and learn how to use it myself. For over a year I have known the agony and ecstasy of this new existence — the agony a computer can put a person through when it isn't working right, and the ecstasy it can provide when it starts accomplishing wonders.

At times I have felt like a pioneer in the wilderness. After its most recent trip back from the serviceman's bench, which it had left working all right, I hooked my video terminal to the computer, turned it on, and found it would print everything — but only in the space of one short line, writing everything over and over that one line. I turned it off and did something I had never done in the course of our love-hate relationship — I raised my hand to it. I jiggled it! Then I turned it on again, and now the cursor, the little bright underline that indicates where the next printed character will appear, showed up in the middle of the screen. Now the lines marched down the screen in perfect order — but only the left half of them showed on the screen.

For some reason connected with desperation I lifted the left edge of the terminal, tilting it sideways. The cursor flickered out and reappeared in its proper place, on the left-hand side of the screen! From then on the terminal worked . . . most of the time. This terminal, however, is already obsolete. I have replaced it with a new "smart" terminal, which has its own microprocessor and is far superior in performance to the earlier model, even when it was working right.

If any aspect of home computers seems undependable or too complicated now, there is little cause for concern, because every month or so seems to bring further simplifications and improvements that make them easier to use. Home computers that combine the digital computer, video terminal, and floppy-disk drive into all-in-one units are becoming common, and less expensive. The time is rapidly approaching when computers will be an essential part of most American homes. Getting acquainted with one has opened my eyes to this coming way of life and left me with a whole new set of questions to ponder as to where we are going. A general understanding of computers will give us all a better chance of going in the right direction.

Contents

HOME COMPUTERS

1

Computers for Everyone

Within ten years some form of computer will be in most American homes. The home computer, personal computer, microcomputer — call it what you will, we are talking about a small computer that will revolutionize our way of life.

Among other things it will be an educator, an entertainer, an inventory expert and file clerk, an assistant chef, a conservationist, a counselor, a personal newspaper and shopping guide, and a string around our finger.

Computers can help us learn anything from algebra to a foreign language, from Chinese history to particle physics. As time goes on, researching a subject by computer will supersede other methods because the user will be able to quickly call up all the material he needs via computer rather than spend days or weeks or months searching it out himself.

As an entertainer the computer has something for every age, taste, and temperament, from tic-tac-toe to chess, from games that simulate sports to games that simulate war. "Do you want me to play my best game?" the computer may ask, giving us a chance to face easier competition until we've raised our own play to a level at which we feel ready to take on the computer's best.

For keeping track of such things as income-tax records, household expenses, and budgets, the computer is an unsurpassed tool. Give it the figures and it will do all those computations that would cover a dozen sheets of paper and consume hours of time and effort if we had to do all the work ourselves.

Anyone can do an inventory of household furnishings, of course, or an inventory of the contents of a safe-deposit box. One goes through the house room by room and notes down every item of value, or one lists every bond, stock certificate, deed, and piece of jewelry in the safe-deposit box. When the inventory is finished it is no more trouble to type up the list than it would be to enter it in the computer.

The only trouble is, life in the average household does not hold still, nor do the contents of most safe-deposit boxes remain unchanged. We discard one piece of furniture and buy another. We put something else in the safe-deposit or take something out. We cross out lines in our inventory and write new entries between the lines in crabbed handwriting that somehow has become illegible by the time we next look at it. After a while the only solution is to try to decipher the mess, retype it, and start all over again.

With a computer we don't cross out lines, we simply make them vanish. There can always be space for new lines. If we wish, we can keep our entries in alphabetical order and always have space for new entries in their proper place. Because our list remains orderly and legible we never have to rewrite it.

The same advantage holds for keeping a permanent and up-to-date "address book" in the computer. People do not stay put these days. A nephew of mine had four different addresses in two years, by which time his page in my address book was a shambles, with arrows pointing to crossed-out addresses running down the margins and with his latest phone number penciled in on top of a largely unsuccessful erasure. The computer has no trouble with such changes. Old addresses can be eliminated or retained, but whatever is done, the entries remain orderly and legible.

"Let me see that recipe for blueberry muffins Aunt Laura sent me." Now it's in the computer. If a recipe in its file is for six servings and we are having ten for dinner, the computer can give us the proportionate amounts of all ingredients needed for ten. It can keep track of cooking time and make sure dinner isn't burned.

The computer can turn off lights and turn down the heat in rooms that are not being used, and otherwise monitor use of fuel, electricity, and water. It can also take care of such chores as turning on lawn sprinklers and turning them off when the lawn has soaked long enough. Computer processes are already being used in automobiles to fine-tune the operations of spark plugs and carbure-tors and get more miles from a gallon of fuel, as well as provide readouts on the dashboard of such information as exactly how many more miles the car can go on the amount of gas left in its tank.

As a counselor a computer can be of great help, since its findings are totally objective and based only on the facts. Of course, if we give it false or faulty information it will draw false conclu-sions, but that is no fault of the computer. For example, a person might want to know which of three possible investments will earn him the best returns in the next five years:

A stock that pays high dividends but whose returns are taxable at both federal and state levels

A U.S. Treasury Bond with a lower return whose divi-dends will be subject to federal but not state income tax

A tax-exempt bond with a still lower return that will not be subject to federal income tax but will be to state income tax

The computations involved in this sort of analysis are enough to ruin an evening for some of us, even if we use an electronic calculator. With a computer all the complicated arithmetic is done in a split second and the same program can be used for various combinations of stocks and bonds.

In its role as a personal newspaper and shopping guide the computer can bring us news reports, stock market reports, super- markets' daily lists of bargains, and other such information selected by the user — as it becomes available. All these functions are technically feasible today; it is only the large-scale ability to link up home computers economically with data-processing cen- ters and data banks that is missing.

Finally, the home computer makes a wonderful aid to those of us who tend to be forgetful.

"Where did we put that box of springs and hooks when we dismantled the screenhouse last fall?" Things my family uses seasonally or rarely have always been the bane of my existence. Each fall when I squirrel away a camp stove or a beach bag I feel sure I will remember where I put it; but when I try to call up those locations the next spring I find that my memory, unlike the computer's, has gone blank.

For more than a year now I have had a home computer to work with, and I am particularly grateful for the endless hours of searching I have been spared. Some of these hours have been spent assembling a Reminders and Locations list in the computer, but they have been hours of enjoyment rather than of irritation and frustration. Like a good secretary, a home computer can bring order out of chaos in a variety of ways, and this alone is a tremendous boon.

It is not the present-day home computer that will make all this a reality in most homes, of course. Today's home computer is the pioneer ancestor of the ones that will be in use a decade from now.

Today's electronic calculators cost a fraction of what early models did and have far greater capabilities. Home computers will follow the same path. They will become more compact yet more powerful, and much simpler to use, and only then will they come into general use. When automobiles first came onto the scene only good mechanics could operate them successfully. Today America is full of people who have been driving cars for forty or fifty years without knowing a distributor from an axle. The home computer will soon take as little knowledge to operate.

But how will the kitchen range, the garage doors, the doorbells, lawn sprinklers, and everything else be hooked up to the computer? New houses can be built with the computer's functions in mind, but to run new wiring all over old houses is a complicated and expensive procedure. Won't that discourage many people from installing computers? Yes, but only until someone comes up with a way to simplify this problem or bypass it. For instance, might not the home computer develop into a sort of small broadcasting system and beam its commands, instructions, and information to computerized apparatus and appliances all over the house? Considering the miracles that have already become commonplace, anything seems possible.

Within ten years computers are going to be living with us, and millions of families will be wondering how they ever managed without them. But as far as living with them is concerned, we have already turned that corner into the Computer Age.

2

Computers We
Already Live With

Computers in the home are inevitable if only because they have already appeared almost everywhere else.

Video terminals, or monitors, are the parts of a computer system the public sees most frequently. These come in a variety of shapes and sizes but usually look like small television sets with a keyboard attached.

The screen may be any size from a few inches wide to half the size of an average TV screen. The keyboard, or *keypad,* may have only a few keys or an array larger than a typewriter's. Each terminal is hooked up to a central computer by either telephone or direct line so that information can be brought to the screen from the computer or sent to the computer by the user of the terminal.

Banking operations would stop today if all computers were removed. Records of many bank transactions are no longer kept in ledgers but on tape or magnetic disks. Somewhere near the central office of any large bank can be found the bank's data-control center, keeping a low profile in a suite of offices to which no great attention is called. Every branch office is tied in to the system; all transactions are recorded there, and all requests for information about customers' balances, deposits, withdrawals, and such matters are automatically handled by the central computer.

One data-control center I visited occupied office space several floors above the bank, in a suite that was no longer large enough to keep pace with the bank's rapidly expanding use of computers. The manager pointed to a line across the middle of the floor in one large room full of equipment.

"That used to be the wall between two rooms. The wall was taken out to double our space — and already we need more."

Externally, computers are not much to look at. Mostly they are large metal boxes with their interesting parts concealed, and even those parts are not very revealing to most of us. Machinery such as printing presses, factory or engine-room equipment, assembly lines, or steel-mill devices can be interesting and even spectacular, because things are moving, things are pumping up and down, sliding sideways, turning, thumping, banging; but in a computer system's insides there is little visible movement and not much sound.

The peripherals, pieces of equipment hooked up to the computer, are often more visually interesting; for example, a printer that can make a "hard copy" of a computer's output. The one I saw was printing thousands of checks, each to a different bank customer for a different amount. All the necessary information was being fed to the check printer by the computer.

The room seemed a bit warmer than I had expected. Computers, like the rest of us, can become cranky if exposed to hot weather. When I commented on the room temperature, the manager nodded.

"You're right." He pointed to a large upright box standing in one corner. "That's a five-ton air conditioner, but it's not adequate anymore. Next week we're replacing it with a ten-ton job."

In its public areas the bank was having the same struggle to keep up with its computer needs. At that time only a single terminal was available to all tellers for checking on accounts and requesting other information. Soon, however, there would be a terminal beside each teller's window.

In the center of the main floor a computerized device had been installed for the use of customers who wished to check their own accounts. The box has a slot for the customer's plastic bank card and a keypad on which his special identification number can be typed. Five bits of information then become available: current balance, date and amount of last deposit, interest earned last quarter, and interest earned to date for the year.

In the bank's outer lobby, open twenty-four hours a day, a fully computerized setup permits a customer to make deposits, transfer money from one account to another, and even draw out cash. Sometimes this type of system includes a recorded voice that asks questions, gives instructions, and otherwise helps the customer complete every phase of his business.

In department stores even older clerks seldom use the term "cash register" anymore if they have the new "point-of-sale terminal" connected to a central computer. Although it is still possible to buy things with actual money, the computer is unquestionably heading us toward a cashless society in which everything we buy will be recorded on "terminals" and will be paid for by transfers of funds from our bank accounts.

The terminal's screen displays instructions that take the clerk step by step through a routine involving a few key numbers that are translated into a printout on a sales slip. The slip describes the article purchased, gives the price, adds the tax, and prints the total.

Each sale is recorded in the data-control center and each item sold is subtracted from the record of the store's total stock of that item. When the supply reaches a predetermined minimum, the computer calls attention to this so that a new supply can be ordered. With this kind of constant inventory review, there is no longer any excuse for clerks' having to say, "Yes, we did have the shirts you want, but we're out of them" — provided the new order comes through on time. Stores used to close once a year for a couple of days to take an annual inventory, and every employer and employee groaned at the thought of all the tedious work involved. Computers enormously simplify this problem.

Computerized cash registers have become standard in supermarkets, and most of the merchandise bears a "zebra number," or "bar code":

When the system is fully operative, the clerk sometimes uses a light pen to check the zebra numbers but more likely runs each item's number across a scanner set into the counter surface. Having identified the item, the register prints out all necessary information about it, including price, and adds the price to a running total. Every sale is noted in a constantly updated inventory of stock.

Despite problems, computers may yet be the salvation of libraries, where endless expansion is unavoidable. A torrent of new books pours in, a trickle of discards leaves. For many libraries, computers and microfilm have come to the rescue just in time.

Newspapers and periodicals, and bound volumes of both, often occupy huge rooms in libraries. Today the same material can be contained on a single shelf. More important, computer techniques make such material more readily available and reduce retrieval time.

The very nature of libraries, however, makes the installation of computer systems especially difficult. Simply entering the contents of the card catalogue into the computer makes no sense, since many books listed there have been lost or stolen. Only the actual books on the shelves or to be returned from circulation belong there. Yet no library can afford the man-hours it would take to enter its collection shelf by shelf, giving each book its individual zebra number.

How difficult computerizing a library can be is illustrated by a story that appeared in the *New York Times:*

> When Princeton University installed a computer in its Firestone Library in January 1977, it described the $150,000 system as the most advanced library computer in the country.
>
> The system checked out books with light pens in much the same way that some supermarkets check out groceries. In addition it was said to give instantaneous information on circulation patterns.
>
> Today the Princeton University library is again using its old 3-by-5-inch manual cardfiling system. "We're still trying to pick up the pieces," says James A. Cogswell, the university's circulation librarian.
>
> The computer system "tended to break down a good deal of the time," he says, with the result that "records were either scrambled, garbled or outright lost" and "a number of records were totally false."

The computer is gone, and Princeton was "hoping to find another computer system that works." The company that built the computer "picked up the tab for the failure and got out of the library-computer business."

One system that seems to be working is used by the Providence (Rhode Island) Public Library. It has been in use for two years but it is still far from including the library's entire collection. New books receive their zebra numbers and are entered in the computer records as they arrive. Old books are given zebra numbers and entered the first time they circulate. But there are worthwhile books in most libraries that nobody has taken out for ten or fifteen years. In the end the only way to complete the records will probably be a shelf-by-shelf search for the stragglers, perhaps by a volunteer group of friends of the library.

Even so, this library computer's accomplishments are already impressive. The zebra number is affixed inside the cover of each book. Another is printed on each patron's library card. Attached to the circulation-desk terminal is a light pen, a tube with a small diode in the end of it. (A diode is an electronic device that allows current to flow in one direction.)

First the patron's card is slipped into a slot on the terminal. The librarian runs the light pen over the zebra number to make sure the patron does not owe an excessive amount in fines on overdue books. She checks the zebra numbers of the books being taken out, causing the computer to record them by author and title and to note the date so that when they are returned it can report whether or not they are overdue and how much is owed.

When I failed to find a book I needed on the shelves, a computer check showed that the book had been taken out three years earlier and not returned. The computer then checked all branch libraries to see if any of them had a copy, found one that did, and asked to have the copy sent to the main library the next day for me to pick up.

At the end of each day the computer records how many books were returned, how many were taken out, how many new patrons were issued library cards, and other useful data. All in all, a far cry from the days when card catalogues and a rubber stamp on the end of a pencil were a librarian's principal tools.

Recently a friend showed me how the computer has changed his life as a newspaperman.

Twenty years ago I would have found him at his desk pounding a typewriter. Fifteen years ago I would have found him still using a typewriter but not pounding it anymore, because by then he was using an electric one. He still has a typewriter, but when I arrived he was not using it. He was sitting alongside his desk at the keyboard of a terminal.

Clear yellow-green type glowed on a soft, dark green background, comfortable to look at and extremely readable. Words appeared on the screen as he wrote, and when he reached the end of a line his next words appeared on a new line without his having to stop to hit a carriage-return key, as one would on a typewriter.

When he finished the article he was writing he changed a word or two in the middle of a sentence. The rest of the line shoved over to make room for the new words, and the part of the line that was pushed off at the end reappeared at the beginning of the next line, which in turn adjusted itself by passing along its overflow to the following line.

"Now let's see how it's going to look in single-column width," he said, and tapped a special key. The lines shimmered together as they reassembled into a narrow column. Among the bits of information simultaneously displayed above the story was the number of inches of space the column would take up in the newspaper.

He stored the article in his personal log in the computer and cleared the screen. Later he would call up the article again, make last-minute revisions, then send it to the composing room.

"You don't have to wait till you're finished to store your copy. If you're writing a long story you can store it paragraph by paragraph if you want to," he said. "When I come in late at night to write a review I always do that, because the power has been known to fail around here, and if you're working on material you haven't stored you lose everything you've written."

When the computer arranges material in column widths it also takes care of "justifying" the column (keeping both edges of the lines of type flush, as they are in this book) and of hyphenating words correctly when a word has to be divided at the end of a line.

In the composing room a reporter's copy is no longer set in type, because it is already "in type." A printout of the story is pasted into place on a page layout and the whole page is photographed for use in offset printing.

Wall Street has of course become heavily computerized. It was not many years ago when a record of each transaction on the New York Stock Exchange reached brokerage offices through a device called a "ticker tape" machine. Number of shares traded, stock symbol, and selling price of each stock were printed on a ribbon of paper tape that came out of the machine in a continuous strip. There was always lots of discarded ticker tape in brokers' wastebaskets. Whenever some famous person was given a hero's welcome in New York City and was driven uptown along Lower Broadway through the financial district, long streamers of ticker tape would fill the air and spiral down from all the office windows to give the hero a real Wall Street welcome.

The ticker tape machine has become a museum piece. Stock-market reports now stream across an electronic panel on the wall. And for detailed information on a specific stock a broker no longer needs to watch the tape or consult reference books. He enters the stock's symbol on the terminal standing on his desk. It then displays the name of the company, its high and low stock prices thus far during the day's trading, its current price, and other up-to-the-minute information.

Twenty years ago the first fully automated post office in the country began operations, and immediately the system made all sorts of mistakes. At first it was likely to accept almost any kind of stamp on a letter. Thrifty jokers had fun sending their holiday greeting cards through the mail with Christmas seals in place of postage stamps. Bit by bit, however, "computer errors" were corrected and the operation became more efficient. (The kind of errors that are generally called "computer errors" are not made by the computer but by the human being who programs it.) Today the same post office handles mail on a regional basis for an area many times larger than the city it once served exclusively. Even the postal scales used by the clerks are computerized, and can compute such things as parcel-post rates to any city or town in any zone in the country, so that the customer doesn't have to wait while the clerk paws through thick directories.

Computers also save us a great deal of time we used to spend in waiting while other people made telephone calls for information, all too often to lines that were busy. For example, a travel agent would have to telephone the airlines in order to make a plane reservation for us. Today he taps keys on a terminal that stands on his desk, finds out immediately if seats are available on the flight we want ("Smoking or nonsmoking section?"), and makes our reservation by computer.

It is obvious that the complicated records hospitals must keep make computers essential, but their use goes far beyond this. They also control X-ray treatments, provide simulations of projected treatment, and monitor surgical procedures. From now on the computer will be with us from the cradle to the grave. Birth records are stored by computers, and few large funeral directors' establishments and cemetery offices are without data-processing systems.

Beauty parlors consult computers for the proper shade of hair dye for a customer. Computer dating services have sprung up everywhere. Some of them are fraudulent (in some cases their "computer data" has proved to consist of a few tattered card files in a back room), but many are bona fide and successful operations. I know of at least one computer match-up that has resulted in a happy marriage.

Schools, colleges, and universities not only keep most of their records by computer but are beginning to feel behind the times if they don't include some sort of computer course in their curriculum. Government agencies, insurance offices, Blue Cross, bookstores, telephone, gas, and electric companies, hotels, museums, radio and television stations — where can we not find computers? It will soon be an old-fashioned doctor or lawyer whose records are not computerized. Even churches depend on computers.

All the computers we have been discussing have one great limitation compared to home computers, however: they are "dedicated" computers designed for a specific use, computers that cannot be used for other purposes. You can't write a program of your own on a travel agent's or a department store's terminal. You can't relax at a stockbroker's terminal by programming it to play backgammon. By contrast, the home computer's possible applications are almost unlimited. In time it will be able to reach out to many of the sources of information we have mentioned and call up on its own terminal whatever data the home user needs — and it is then that the home computer will come into its own.

Computers, then, vary greatly, but in one respect they are all alike. Large or small, they must have the same two things to work with in order to function: hardware and software.

3

Hardware

The physical parts of a computer system, those made of silicon and plastic, glass and metal, are called *hardware*. Integrated circuits, memory boards, keyboards, video terminals, floppy-disk drives, all such components of the system are its hardware.

Software refers to the computer's programs, operating instructions, and lists of information. One might think of an automobile as "hardware" and the driver's actions as "software." By itself, an automobile is an inert mass of metal, plastic, glass, and rubber, unable to do anything; it must have a driver. The driver's actions "program" the car. On the other hand, the driver can put his programming abilities to use only when he has the physical hardware called a car at his disposal.

Without hardware there would be no computer. Without software a computer would be useless.

A working home-computer system includes at the minimum a cassette tape recorder, a digital computer, and a video terminal.

For the moment let's think of these three units in simple terms as a storeroom, a workshop, and a showroom. The tape recorder functions as a storeroom, since computer programs can be recorded and stored on tape. The computer itself is the workshop in which programs are put to use, and the screen of the video terminal is the showroom where the final product is displayed.

Like materials brought from a storeroom into a workshop, programs can be loaded into the computer from a tape recorder. At the same time, the computer is not limited to using pre-programmed material. It is also prepared to handle programs written directly into it, or to be used as a "scratch pad" when an immediate answer to a computation is desired. And if a user writes a program of his own that he wishes to save, the computer can send it to the tape recorder for storage.

Any programmed material fed into the computer is stored in its memory, but that storage is only temporary, and is also limited. Storage lasts only as long as the computer stays on. Turn it off, and the programmed material is lost. But even if the computer could retain your programs, it would soon run out of storage space. In a home computer with a modest amount of memory a single program, if it is exceptionally long, may result in a message something like this:

OUT OF RAM SPACE AT LINE 30

— meaning that the computer does not have room enough to handle it. (We will talk about the meaning of RAM later.) Some form of outside storage space is essential.

The computer has a good deal of built-in programming equipment, including lists of instructions for handling general programs; translating capability for the conversion of one computer language into another; routines for dealing with arithmetic and logic problems; and other tools without which it could not begin operation. To make use of the impulses it picks up from a tape or the instructions and data it receives from a user, it must translate this "input" into machine language it can understand, into instructions and commands it can then execute.

All this essential material is programmed into the computer by the manufacturer and is etched permanently into the computer's memory so that it remains intact whether the power is on or off. This memory is called *ROM*, or *read-only memory*. ROM may be read but may not be written into (may not have anything added to it or deleted from it) or be otherwise changed in any way. ROM programs, though software in one sense, thus become part of the hardware as well. In recognition of this, ROM is sometimes called *firmware*.

As a workshop the computer is now equipped to receive and run programs. The user writes new programs on the video terminal, which will be described in detail later. Whatever the user writes appears on the screen as it enters the computer. This material is called "input." Anything the computer sends to the screen is called "output."

Each line of a new program is stored temporarily in the computer's *RAM* (*random-access memory*). To explain the term RAM we can compare its storage and retrieval abilities with those of tape. Suppose there are twenty programs on a tape. We might say it has those programs "stored in its memory." To get to the twentieth one, we have to run the tape forward all the way past the first nineteen. A tape recorder has only sequential access to its programs.

The computer has random access to its memory. Given a command that identifies a program, it can go directly to the area where that program is stored and produce it.

The computer's "workshop" is divided into five compartments:

1.   Accumulators
2.   Control

3.   Arithmetic/logic unit
4.   Data register (storage)
5.   Memory address register

The first three are gathered in what has been called the heart of the computer and its nerve center as well, the *CPU* (*central processing unit*). In appearance it is a small and inconspicuous part of one of the circuit boards inside the computer, but it is a mighty mite. Here is where the *accumulators* gather bits of material brought out of memory and store them temporarily within the CPU itself. Here the *ALU* (*arithmetic/logic unit*) stands ready to perform mathematical and logic functions. As for *Control*, its operations resemble those of a traffic cop at a busy intersection or the controller of a railroad switchyard.

With signals arriving in microseconds from all directions the timing must be exact. Built into the CPU or located on the chip of a nearby integrated circuit is the computer "clock," which sends out pulses at a rate of between two million and four million beats per second. With this kind of timing at its command, Control makes sure that the accumulated data, instructions, and other material appear in the proper sequence.

The *data register* (memory or storage) department is where the bulk of information is temporarily stored. The *memory address register* keeps track of the location of each bit of information in a computer's memory.

All this activity takes place inside a black metal box in which nothing visibly moves. The computer has no moving parts.

The digital computer shown on page 23 is about sixteen inches square and a little over six inches high. Inside, slanted at an angle toward the back of the box, are a number of circuit boards, including memory boards.

All these boards are interconnected, and all information and instructions travel by way of electronic circuits.

In our home electric circuits, current flows through wires to lamps, toasters, radios, TV sets, shavers, hair dryers, refrigerators, air conditioners, and everything else that uses electricity. It travels through wires that, by electronic standards, are monstrous. In computers the current travels along miniaturized printed electronic circuits. The IC's (*integrated circuit chips*) that contain these printed circuits are what have made it possible to reduce so dramatically the size of computers. IC's are silicon chips about a quarter of an inch square, or less, upon which have been etched and imprinted several layers of electronic circuitry.

A tiny current travels along this circuitry, controlled by a multitude of "gates," or "flip-flops." These electronic switches either open to stop the current's flow or to switch it to another direction, or close to let it pass through. Millions of these gates are involved in a circuit; which ones open and which close depends on what we are asking the computer to do.

Programs can be fed into a computer without the use of a video terminal and its keyboard, but such programs would consist mostly

Digital computer (right) and floppy-disk drive. A second drive can be installed in the right-hand compartment

of a series of numbers entered from the computer's keyboard. Here are a few lines of such a program:

> Press Memory Key, then enter:
> 040 100
> Press Alter Key, then enter:
> 041
> 160
> 040
> 021
> 260 . . .

After making fifty more such entries we have a program that, when run, produces over three hundred numbers in a certain sequence, which indicate that the computer is operating properly. This is good news, but otherwise not a very stimulating experience.

Most of us want a display we can read and understand, and for that we need a video terminal where anything we write or anything the computer produces appears on what looks like a small TV screen, as shown on page 25.

Attached to the frame that houses the screen and the terminal's other hardware is a keyboard like that on a typewriter. Any letters or symbols we type on this keyboard appear on the screen as we type them.

Much of the hardware inside the terminal is like that found in TV consoles. In fact, a TV set can be hooked up to the computer for use as a monitor, but this is seldom popular with other members of the family who want to watch their favorite programs.

The home computer is a jack-of-all-trades whose possibilities are limited only by the user's imagination. Nothing we write into the computer, no unworkable instruction we may give it, is going to injure it or cause it to blow a fuse. The only damage we are likely to do is to our own programs; a wrong course of action can lose whatever material we have in the computer at the moment, but no other harm will be done.

Sitting down at the keyboard for the first time is like opening a five-pound box of chocolates. All sorts of interesting functions are at your fingertips just waiting to be tried.

Just as on a typewriter there is a Shift key, since many of the keys control two symbols, even though on some home computers the alphabet appears only in uppercase letters. On one key, for example, there is a small arrow pointing up. A shift on that key produces a caret, $\wedge$, which is used to raise a number to any power desired. For example:

(For 2^2)   PRINT 2$\wedge$2   The computer prints 4
(For 3^3)   PRINT 3$\wedge$3   The computer prints 27
(For 8^7)   PRINT 8$\wedge$7   The computer prints 2.09715E+06

Video terminals: the old "dumb" terminal (left) and the new "smart" one. The new terminal can put lines on the screen sixteen times as fast as the old one

The "smart" video terminal's keyboard. Both uppercase and lowercase letters are available

In the last figure the E indicates *exponential notation*, which expresses a figure as a decimal number raised to a power of 10. "E + 06" means that the decimal point in the figure should be moved six places to the right. This would give us 2097150. The exact figure would be 2097152, but the computer rounds off both whole numbers and decimal fractions after six places.

Among the other special keys besides the Shift key are: "Delete," with which we can back up to erase a wrong letter or misspelled word and replace it with a correction; "Repeat," which, if held down with another key, will cause that key's letter or symbol to repeat as many times as we wish; "Scroll," which moves lines upward one at a time; "Erase," which will clear the screen; and "Return," which works like the carriage return on a typewriter, bringing the cursor back and down to the beginning of a new line.

There is a >, which means "more than," and a <, which means "less than": 8>3 means "8 is more than 3," 8<3 means "8 is less than 3." As you will notice, the first statement is true, the second is false. These symbols are useful, since the computer accepts true statements and ignores false ones. Programs are often controlled by true and false statements, as we shall see later.

Besides the individual keys there are combinations that produce interesting results. A key marked "Ctrl" is used for various Control combinations; for example, Control-C. If a program is running, or a listing of the program's lines, and we have seen all we need to, holding down Ctrl and C simultaneously will cause the program to break off. Control-S will halt it at any point, and Control-Q will cause it to continue.

The home computer provides us with a versatile set of tools, but nothing can be done with them until the computer and its user have a language to work with. This has to be provided by a peripheral device.

Any device attached to the computer is a "peripheral." The word means "located away from a center or central portion." The terminal is a peripheral, and so is the tape recorder, which can provide the language that makes the computer usable.

A more efficient memory and storage device, however, is the

floppy disk, which allows for direct retrieval of material, uses EXTENDED BASIC (a computer language; see pages 45 to 52), and greatly expands the computer's capabilities. If I thought the floppy-disk devices were going to remain as expensive as they are now (they may cost more than the computer itself), I would not dwell on them here, but this will not be the case. Already a desk-top computer system that includes computer, terminal, and floppy-disk drive all in a single unit is on the market at a price lower than that of the three individual units.

Floppy disks come by their name honestly. The minidisks used in home computers are flexible plastic disks 5¼ inches in diameter that look like some strange kind of phonograph record (see page 29). They come in square paper jackets that are never removed. A section of the disk is exposed by a slot in the jacket, through which the read/write head makes contact and "plays" the disk when it has been inserted into the floppy-disk drive. The disk is coated with magnetic material on which data can be recorded rapidly in large quantities. When it's being "played," the almost frictionless surface of the disk revolves at high speed inside the jacket.

Unlike phonograph records, floppy disks do not have a single spiral track. Their grooves consist of concentric circles. This means that the outside tracks are much longer than those near the center, but the same amount of information is stored on each track because each segment must be equal as far as the amount of information it holds is concerned. This is not the most efficient arrangement. Something better will eventually be developed to make more complete use of potential storage space; but the ability of the floppy disk's read/write head to go directly to the segment called for — its random-access capability — makes it a powerful tool.

In appearance the floppy-disk device is another black box,

Floppy disks, and an interior view of the disk drive

slightly smaller than the computer (see above). It can contain one drive or two. With two disk drives, material can easily be transferred from one disk to another and programs can be called up from either disk. With slightly more effort, however, the same transfers can be made with a single drive. For most home users this is quite adequate.

Other peripherals include *printers*, for those who want a printed copy of what appears on the screen. For instance, suppose you want to keep a daily or weekly record of the current value of a portfolio of stocks and bonds. A program can be set up into which you enter the day's quotations for each stock, after which you get a complete listing of each stock's number of shares, price, and current total value. Each time the program is used, however, the previous list is cleared out to make way for the new listings. With a printer, each day's list can be preserved.

Special typewriters can also be tied in to the computer system. With these you can write a letter on the terminal and then instruct the typewriter to type as many copies as you wish. If you have included in your programmed instructions a list of the people you want the letter to go to, each copy will have a different salutation — "Dear Mr. Smith," "Dear Mr. Jones," and so on.

Although nothing seems more modern, the computer was invented nearly one hundred fifty years ago. It existed in the mind of an English scientist, a mathematical genius named Charles Babbage (1792–1871). Had workable hardware been a possibility then, he would have had little trouble providing the software.

Babbage tried to build his computer, and might have succeeded had the arts of metalworking and machine-tooling been more advanced than they were. His machine needed hundreds of gears and shafts, cams and ratchets, and they needed to be constructed with greater accuracy than was possible in those days. His grasp of possibilities ran well ahead of the limitations of his machine shop.

The machine he first began work on grew ever more complex in design. He called it a Difference Engine, because it was a device for calculating mathematical differences. If he had completed his machine it would have been a two-ton monster, but he abandoned it because he had ideas for an "analytical engine" with infinitely greater capacities.

The new concept involved the ideas of programming, sequential control, a "mill" for mathematical computations, memory, and an automatic readout or display of the results — all the operations of a modern computer: input, control, computing, memory, and output.

Despite a valiant try, Babbage's machine never got built. There is every reason to think it would have worked, however, or that if it had not worked at first he would have "debugged" it and got it going in the end.

Babbage should have been born in the twentieth century. He would have loved it here. One computer expert went so far as to say, "If Babby were alive today, I'd be out of a job."

Many important inventions started small and became bigger. The Wright Brothers' first airplane was a gnat compared to today's 747s and Concordes. George Stephenson's "Rocket," the first railroad engine, was a toy compared to the giant locomotives that followed. Today's trailer trucks could carry several of the earliest motor trucks.

Electronic equipment, however, has gone the other way. Early computers that filled whole rooms are outperformed today by tabletop models. Nor is size the only thing that has shrunk. Prices have shrunk and will continue to do so. In the 1960s a computer with the capabilities of home computers today would have cost $50,000, nearly a hundred times the price of many of today's models.

Babbage's computer with its mechanical parts would have been an exceedingly slow performer by today's standards. For that matter, so were the first computers built back in World War II days. Some were huge affairs, as much as a hundred feet long. These were "analog" computers, which operated differently from digital computers. Digital computers are "counters"; they make exact calculations. Analog computers make comparisons; they are "measuring sticks" rather than counters, and are more limited in what they can accomplish. The gas gauge on a car is an analog device. It reproduces on a small scale the amount of space still occupied by fuel in the gas tank.

Military needs in World War II gave scientists the opportunities and the backing they needed to produce ENIAC (Electronic Numberial Integrator and Computer), the first electronic digital computer. Developed in 1944–46 at the University of Pennsylvania, ENIAC was a thirty-ton giant that used twenty thousand vacuum tubes. Because the tubes tended to have very short lives, problems with ENIAC were formidable, but it became a powerful weapon capable of computations concerning new armament that unquestionably helped win the war.

In ENIAC days scarcely anyone suspected that the computer's future would be revolutionized by one of the most plentiful and commonplace materials on earth: silicon. There are enormous quantities of silicon around. Beaches are covered with it in the form of sand. It is the most abundant element next to oxygen in the earth's crust.

The silicon crystals used for circuit chips, however, are "grown" in laboratories. Crystals whose purity comes within one-tenth of one percent of perfection are created there. Wafers of silicon almost as thin as a page of this book are sliced from crystalline cylinders about three inches in diameter, then carefully polished.

As many as ninety chips one-quarter-inch square can be cut from one of these wafers and many more than that of the smaller sizes. Some chips are as small as one-tenth inch to a side, and some are rectangular rather than square. These are the blanks that will eventually contain a maze of electronic circuits as complicated as the electric wiring in an entire city block.

Engineers first work out a diagram of the network of circuits along which the electric current will travel, a diagram the size of a large tabletop, which is then photographed and reduced on film to the size of the chips being manufactured. (The entire Bible, every page of it, can be placed on a piece of microfilm the size of a business card. The development of microphotography is one of the things that made the silicon chip possible on such a small scale.)

The layout of the circuitry looks like a vast railroad switchyard except that trains could never make it around the right-angle turns involved. As many microfilm copies of this diagram as one three-inch wafer can hold are reproduced side by side, row after row, on one piece of film, and this "mask" is laid over the wafer and used in the process of etching the circuits into the chips by means of ultraviolet light. Silicon is a semiconductor of electricity; it can be either electrically conducting or nonconducting depending on how its surface has been "doped" with other materials (coated or treated with them, that is). On each chip some microscopic areas are treated, others are not, according to what the engineers want the current to do at that point.

The pattern that has now been etched into the chip becomes one layer of its circuitry. Many more layers will be piled on top of this one before the chip is encapsulated in plastic and ready for use.

To appreciate the advantages offered by the silicon chip we must go back to the early computers, whose circuitry, composed of wires, switches, and vacuum tubes, filled whole rooms. These computers could not do one-tenth of what our home computer, using tiny silicon chips, can do. The chip is cheap, tough, dependable, and versatile. And the distances that streams of electrons have to travel along its minuscule circuits are tiny. In earlier computers electricity had to travel through miles of wires. It now travels a few inches in minute amounts to accomplish the same purposes. In the course of millions of trips during the running of a program the saving in time and energy is tremendous.

So far I have tried to give some idea of how the hardware functions. Not until we add the software, however, can we really begin to answer the all-important question, how do computers work?

4

Software

All communication with computers is based on the two instructions that any electrical device can understand and execute: ON and OFF. All computer operations and languages are based on those two opposites, which may be expressed in several ways:

ON	OFF
1	0
Yes	No
True	False
Bridge	No Bridge

In a sense we provide the "software" for every electrical device we use. By flipping up a wall switch to turn on the lights in a room we provide the instruction that activates the hardware. Inside the switch box a gap in a circuit is bridged, so that electricity can travel to the light bulbs. When we flip the switch down the bridge swings away, the circuit is broken, and the lights go off.

Today's computer circuitry involves millions of points where ON/OFF decisions are made, where some form of switch must be able to break the circuit or close it. Since these switches operate billions of times at billionths-of-a-second speeds, no mechanical switch with moving parts could do the work. Early computers used electronic tubes, vacuum tubes, such as were used in old-fashioned radios. In these tubes a near-vacuum was created through which electrons could move easily. The heavy demands made on the tubes, however, were often more than they could handle. They had a bad habit of blowing out at critical moments. The amount of electricity it took to operate the early computers was large, and so was the amount of heat generated.

Heat is still a problem for computers but to a much lesser degree, especially when one takes into account the amount of work they can do. The difference, of course, lies in the extreme miniaturization of circuits that has taken place. In the microcircuits of our computer only a few electrons at a time can squeeze through the maze, but only a few are needed to flip the switches, or "gates," that control the circuit.

In some respects a computer plays an enlarged version of an old parlor game. Instead of playing Twenty Questions it plays Twenty Million Questions, and instead of taking a few seconds to answer a question it can make a million YES/NO choices in a split second. It can respond to each ON/OFF situation in a millisecond or a microsecond or even a nanosecond.

A *millisecond* is a thousandth of a second.

A *microsecond* is a millionth of a second.

A *nanosecond* is a billionth of a second.

Computer people now also talk in terms of *picoseconds,* which are one trillionth of a second. A trillion is a million million, or 1,000,000,000,000.

Imagine millions of tiny electric light bulbs going on and off in response to a string of electrons traveling along microscopic circuits at close to the speed of light. Or think of a railway switch. Throw the switch and the train will curve off onto another track, leave it as is and the train will go straight ahead. The train responds to a YES/NO decision: "Yes, go straight ahead" or "No, turn onto the other track."

When a computer tackles a problem in arithmetic it uses only 1 and 0, 1 being ON and 0 being OFF. Given these two choices it must use the binary system, a system that can represent any number by a combination of 1's and 0's. Once one understands this system one can understand how computers work.

For our own arithmetic we use the decimal system. The decimal (or "base ten") system is based on multiples of ten:

$$
\begin{array}{ll}
1 & \\
10 & (10 \times 1) \\
100 & (10 \times 10 \times 1) \\
1000 & (10 \times 10 \times 10 \times 1)
\end{array}
$$

Each time a number moves one column to the left it is multiplied by ten:

1000	100	10	1
			1
		1	0
	1	0	0
1	0	0	0

In the decimal system we are not limited to 1 or 0 but can use any digit from 1 to 9 and, of course, 0. For example, 8463 is 8000, 400, 60, and 3:

1000	100	10	1
			3
		6	0
	4	0	0
8	0	0	0

Similarly, 7849 would be:

1000	100	10	1
			9
		4	0
	8	0	0
7	0	0	0

When we add these two numbers together this is what happens:

$$
\begin{array}{r}
3 \\
60 \\
400 \\
8000 \\
9 \\
40 \\
800 \\
7000 \\
\hline
12 \\
100 \\
1200 \\
15000 \\
\hline
16312
\end{array}
$$

In the binary system the columns have different values. Instead of multiplying by ten, each column after the first one multiplies by two:

16	8	4	2	1
0	0	0	0	1

Let's begin with the number 1, shown above. It is represented as 01 — or 00001, as shown, or 000000001 — the number of zeros in front of it does not matter.

The number 2 equals 2 times 1, so it is represented in the 2 column with 0 in the 1 column:

16	8	4	2	1
0	0	0	1	0

If we left the 1 in the 1 column we would have a binary number representing 3, since one 2 plus one 1 equals 3:

16	8	4	2	1
0	0	0	1	1

Since the next column to the left multiplies by 4, a 1 in that column represents the number 4:

16	8	4	2	1
0	0	1	0	0

Each number can be represented by some combination of multiples of 2, plus 1 if necessary:

> 5 is 4 plus 1
> 6 is 4 plus 2
> 7 is 4 plus 2 plus 1
> 8 has its own column
> 9 is 8 plus 1
> 10 is 8 plus 2

Our difficulty in understanding the binary system stems from our long association with the decimal system. Instead of multiplying by ten as we move from right to left in the columns, in the binary system we multiply by two — this is easy to say but hard to grasp. When "10" has always stood for ten it is hard to think of it as standing for two. When "100" has always been a hundred it is hard to give it a value of four. But when we look at binary 1's and 0's and add up the columns in which they appear we can begin to understand the system:

16	8	4	2	1	
		0	0	1	(1)
		0	1	0	(2)
		0	1	1	(3)
	0	1	0	0	(4)
	0	1	0	1	(5)
	0	1	1	0	(6)
	0	1	1	1	(7)
0	1	0	0	0	(8)
0	1	0	0	1	(9)
0	1	0	1	0	(10)

Let us hope this begins to make sense. But what good are these figures unless we can use them to add, subtract, multiply, and divide? We can — but the computer solves all arithmetic problems, including subtraction, multiplication, and division, through various methods of addition, so we must begin with addition itself.

If the computer were programmed to demonstrate the binary system by solving a simple problem in arithmetic such as adding 6 and 5, it would go at it this way:

	8	4	2	1	
	0	1	0	1	(5)
+	0	1	1	0	(6)
	1	0	1	1	(11)

(Decimal values: 8 + 0 + 2 + 1 = 11)

Whenever two 1's occur in the same column, as in the 4 column here, their sum equals the value of the next column to the left. Therefore, they add up to 10. We write down 0 and carry 1.

If there are already two 1's in that next column, then the three 1's add up to 11 (10 + 1). We write down 1 and carry 1. This is illustrated when we add 7 and 7:

	8	4	2	1
	0	1	1	1
+	0	1	1	1
	1	1	1	0

If asked to add 5 + 6 + 7, the computer would not add up all three numbers at one time. It adds up numbers two at a time no matter how long a column of figures it is given. This is how it would add 5 + 6 + 7:

+	0	0	1	0	1	(5)
	0	0	1	1	0	(6)
+	0	1	0	1	1	(11)
	0	0	1	1	1	(7)
	1	0	0	1	0	(18)

It is to avoid carrying over more than one 1 at a time from column to column that a computer adds up numbers two at a time.

Since we are not computers we find the binary system slow and cumbersome. For us, 1000000, which is one million in our decimal system, seems a ponderous way to represent 64:

64	32	16	8	4	2	1
1	0	0	0	0	0	0

Long strings of 1's and 0's are confusing, and some of the computer's arithmetic seems primitive. To multiply 25 × 16 it adds up sixteen 25's. We could get the answer that way in the decimal system, too, and even use the computer's two-by-two method:

$$+\ \frac{\begin{array}{r}25\\25\end{array}}{}$$

$$+\ \frac{\begin{array}{r}50\\25\end{array}}{}$$

$$+\ \frac{\begin{array}{r}75\\25\end{array}}{}$$

$$100\ \ldots$$

And so on. But what a system! And doing subtraction and division would be just as cumbersome. The fact that the computer can handle binary numbers millions of times faster than we can is what makes the system practicable, and makes computers work.

All languages are in a sense codes. One of the definitions given for the word "code" is "any system of symbols for meaningful communication." Numbers and alphabets are both systems of symbols. To communicate with the computer, what we need is a code. We employ the binary system to produce that code.

As we know, binary digits are either 1 or 0. Each 1 or 0 is called a *bit*, which is a short form of "binary digit." My computer, like most home computers, uses an eight-bit code. Eight bits are called a *byte* and four bits, or half a byte, are called a *nibble*, or *nybble*. (Perhaps one of these days two bits will become known as a nyp.)

Using the eight-bit code system, code numbers are assigned to each symbol the computer uses. Only seven of the bits are used for the code. The first bit is reserved for additional information that may have to be given about the symbol; for example, whether a number is plus or minus.

Here are 1, 2, 3 in the computer's code:

011 0001	(1)
011 0010	(2)
011 0011	(3)

Here are A, B, C:

100 0001	(A)
100 0010	(B)
100 0011	(C)

If you asked the computer to print the code number of "C" in decimal it would print "67," having converted its code number:

64	32	16	8	4	2	1
1	0	0	0	0	1	1

Every symbol that is used, from punctuation marks to math symbols, has its code number, as for example:

D	O	E	S	6
100 0100	100 1111	100 0101	101 0011	011 0110
+	3	=	9	?
010 1011	011 0011	011 1101	011 1001	011 1111

The computer is something like a printer working with a case of type. In the old days when type was set by hand each letter, number, and other symbol had its own compartment in a typecase. If the compositor wanted a capital R he took a piece of type from the compartment that held capital R's. Part of his training was to memorize the location of each symbol's compartment.

When the computer receives a code number, say, 100 0100, it stores the number in its memory. When called on to reproduce the coded symbol, it finds that the compartment labeled 100 0100 in its "typecase" contains the letter D. It then transmits this letter to the screen.

This is only the beginning of the computer's education. The next trick is the hard one: teaching the computer whole words and expressions and mathematical equations it can understand.

5

Computer Language

In the first computers the binary system was directly employed. Binary numbers were programmed into the computer by means of a series of toggle switches on the front panel. But endless strings of 1's and 0's are boring to enter, and with no visual display of the numbers it was hard not to make mistakes.

This direct approach is called *machine language*, and the programs are called *object programs*. Machine language is the only language the computer can understand, but the programmer no longer has to know how to use it. Machine-language instructions programmed into its ROM enable the computer to convert other languages into machine language.

An intermediate step between machine language and high-level languages such as BASIC is *assembly language*, which makes use of symbols to represent instructions. Programs written in assembly language are translated by the computer into machine-language object programs before they can be used. Assembly language is more difficult than high-level languages but easier to use than machine language. Programs written in languages other than machine language are called *source programs*, being the source of object programs. The computer translates and executes source programs in fractions of a second.

High-level languages are written in words and symbols we can readily understand. A program designed to act as an interpreter converts high-level languages into machine language. The computer is given a list of instructions that might be called a short course in How to Understand and Speak English — or some other language. The computer does not learn the language thoroughly. It is rather like those tourists who go to a foreign country armed with a phrase book, having learned just enough words and phrases to ask directions, order a meal, and cope with taxi drivers. The computer's English is limited to specific commands and instructions. It understands PRINT, STOP, RUN, LIST, SAVE, and it is programmed to respond to our mistakes with error messages such as these:

! ERROR - SYNTAX ERROR

! ERROR - CAN'T FIND VARIABLE MENTIONED IN NEXT STATEMENT

! ERROR - ?02 DEVICE IS NOT CAPABLE OF THIS OPERATION

Many high-level languages have been developed, but the language used in most home computers is some version of BASIC (Beginner's All-Purpose Symbolic Instruction Code). In time it will be superseded by even easier languages, but it has served computers well in their early stages. Other high-level languages whose names may be familiar are COBOL and FORTRAN. COBOL is specifically suited to business use. It is the principal language used by the bank data-control center I visited. FORTRAN is used in scientific work. None of the specialized languages, however, is as generally useful as BASIC.

BASIC was developed in 1965 at Dartmouth College by J. G. Kemeny and T. E. Kurtz, with help from several graduate students. One unfortunate thing about BASIC, however, is that it is now spoken in a hundred different dialects. Each of the many home computers on the market has its own version of BASIC. No effort has been made to set a single standard. A program written for one computer must be adapted to the other's dialect before it can be run in another company's model. Software such as tapes produced for one computer cannot be used with another. As home computers become more common, however, this situation will inevitably change. By the time they become commonplace we will probably give them most of our orders vocally and very simply.

There are several levels of BASIC. The level used by a home computer is governed by its capacity, by how many bytes it is able to accommodate. TINY BASIC can operate on 2K of memory. K equals one *kilobyte,* which roughly equals 1000 bytes — 1024, to be exact. A capacity of 2K is sufficient for a variety of games and educational programs involving relatively simple calculations. BASIC needs 4K, while EXTENDED BASIC calls for 12K.

I have three memory boards in my computer, each with 8K capacity, for a total of 24K, so that I can use the floppy-disk system and EXTENDED BASIC. My variety of BASIC will necessarily be one "dialect." Some of its commands and functions and instructions will be identical to those used by other makes of home computer, while some will be slightly different.

In considering the way a computer makes decisions, it helps to remember that there are only two possibilities, which we can think of as "Yes" and "No," or "True" and "False." Here, for example, is a simple program.

In BASIC programs, each line is numbered, and usually by tens (I will explain why later):

```
10 A = 4
20 IF A = 2 + 3 THEN PRINT "2 + 3 = 4"
30 IF A = 2 + 2 THEN PRINT "2 + 2 = 4"
```

The computer prints:

$$2 + 2 = 4$$

Line 20: The computer has added 2 and 3 and found that the total does not equal A. Therefore it ignores this false statement and goes on to the next line.

Line 30: Here it finds that 2 + 2 does equal A, and since the statement is true it follows the instructions given and prints "2 + 2 = 4."

But suppose we write the program this way, using the symbol <>, which means "does not equal":

```
10 A = 4
20 IF A <> 2 + 2 THEN PRINT "A DOES NOT EQUAL 4"
30 IF A <> 2 + 3 THEN PRINT "A DOES NOT EQUAL 5"
```

The computer prints:

A DOES NOT EQUAL 5

Line 20: Since A does equal 2 + 2, line 20's statement is false.

Line 30: Since A does not equal 2 + 3, line 30's statement is true.

The computer ignores line 20 and prints line 30's *string literal*. Any string of words, or words and figures, enclosed in quotation marks and preceded by the instruction PRINT, is printed literally as it is given, hence the term "string literal." If we wrote the following lines:

```
10 A = 2 + 2
20 PRINT A
```

The computer would print:

4

The expression 2 + 2 is not a string literal, and therefore the computer treats it as an arithmetic problem and prints the sum. If the expression were written in string-literal form (A = "2 + 2"), then the computer would print 2 + 2.

The computer considers each line of a program in turn, and does what it is told *if the instruction given is valid.* If the instruction given cannot be carried out, the computer ignores it and goes on to the next line.

How does the computer move from one space to the next? To begin with, it gives us a prompt mark on the screen. Beside the prompt mark, which is an asterisk, appears a single-character underline called a *cursor.* This moves along one space ahead of whatever we type on the screen, indicating where the next character is to appear. Writing the command RUN would proceed like this (visualize the letters as appearing in sequence on the same line):

*_

*R_

*RU_

*RUN_

RUN is the command given when we have written a program and want the computer to execute it. To begin a new line, as we learned in chapter three, we hit the Return key. In this instance, however, we would hit the Return key in order to cause execution of the command RUN.

Besides being used for the writing or running of programs, a computer can be used as a scratch pad for quick calculations. Incidentally, it has its plus and minus signs, but it uses * for multiplication and / for division. The reason for using the asterisk instead of × is that a computer cannot tell when × is meant to be a letter and when it is meant to be a times sign (one place, at least, where we're smarter than it is).

Suppose we want to know something simple, like the answer to 11823 times 47 divided by 563 plus 3482? We don't need to write a program for that. Instead we start with the command PRINT:

PRINT 11823*47/563+3482

Then we hit the Return key, and immediately get the answer:

4469

Nothing wonderful about that, of course. We could do it just as fast or faster on a calculator. What I like about the computer, though, is that all the figures stay put where I can see them and make sure I entered them correctly. At the same time it is important to understand that a computer is *not* a calculator in the same totally accurate sense. It has that habit of rounding off figures after six places. Keep your bank balance under $10,000 and you will have a faultless bookkeeper. Get your balance up to $10,000.23 and it will hand you back 10000.2; and should you be fortunate enough to bank $100,000.23 you will lose the whole 23¢. The obvious remedy is to round off your balance if it goes above six figures.

When using the scratch pad the temptation to fool around becomes, of course, irresistible. Knowing that early computers panicked and stopped working when asked to divide a figure by zero, it is only natural to type, "PRINT 4/0," and sit back to wait for the fireworks. Hitting the Return key, however, merely produces ! ERROR - ATTEMPTED DIVIDE BY ZERO. And "PRINT SQR(−1)," which asks for the impossible, the square root of −1, is brushed aside with an ! ERROR - ILLEGAL NUMBER VALUE. Computers have become more sophisticated.

As new lines appear, those above them move up the screen and scroll off at the top. When we doodle with other problems the two lines of our first problem move up and disappear. When they leave the screen they are gone forever. The computer does not waste its memory on anything but programmed material, so we must make a note of that "4469" before it gets away.

Commands and instructions given in the scratch-pad style are executed at once. To indicate we are writing a program that is not to be executed in any part until we have finished writing all of it, we number each line. To show that we have completed the program we type a final line giving the command STOP or END. In programming, lines are usually numbered by tens. This leaves room to insert new lines in the program later on, if we decide to change or refine it.

Each time a line is completed the programmer taps the Return key. This causes the prompt mark and cursor to appear at the left-hand edge of the next line. Each numbered line is stored in memory. Even though lines scroll off the screen as the program lengthens, they are retained. When the program is complete the command LIST will cause it to reappear line by line, in numerical order, and the command RUN will cause the program to be executed. If the programmer has made an error in line 90 the computer will stop execution at that line and give him an error message for line 90. When line 90 has been debugged, and if there are no more errors, the program will then run smoothly to the end and provide whatever output is expected. New lines written out of numerical order automatically take their proper place in the lineup when the program is run or listed.

A program of any size and complexity seldom works out exactly right the first time you write it. Perhaps an instruction or series of instructions you thought would accomplish one thing turns out to accomplish something quite different and not at all what you had in mind. Or perhaps you have the right instructions but have entered them in slightly wrong order. Let's see now . . . instead of that, suppose we tried this? . . .

If you enjoy a game of wits, problem solving, and detective work, then you will enjoy working out your own programs.

6

▪▪

Programming
the Computer

Most people who buy home computers in the future will not be interested in writing programs themselves. They will want a push-button affair with ready-made programs to do the work. But no computer game or ready-made program can provide half the fun of working out programs for ourselves.

Almost anything can happen when we are first learning, but no matter what we type on the keyboard the computer will not suddenly blow up or collapse into a smoking ruin. In most cases it will simply point out our mistakes and wait for us to correct them. For instance, suppose we wrote this:

PRIINT "I AM A STUPID COMPUTER"

The computer would click and print,

! ERROR - SYNTAX ERROR

—not because its feelings were hurt but because we had not spelled the command PRINT correctly. Syntax usually pertains to sentence structure and the arrangement of words, but another of its meanings is simply "orderly arrangement," and that is what the computer is driving at. The computer is all for orderly arrangement. It won't tolerate anything less. Any mistake we make is called firmly to our attention, and everything stops until we either correct it or change the subject.

When the instruction has been retyped with PRINT spelled correctly the screen will display:

I AM A STUPID COMPUTER

You can't insult a computer. Nothing bothers it. It never shows emotion or feelings of any kind. This is what makes it such an effective teaching aid. If a student tries to add up a small column of figures and gets a wrong answer five times running, a human teacher needs to be superhuman to remain patient. But the computer will let a user miss the answer any number of times and simply keep telling him to try again. It never suggests that he or she is dumb. It is infinitely patient. And if Cousin Hazel (who never had much of a head for figures, by her own admission) is trying her hand at it, the computer can be programmed to say, ATTAGIRL, HAZEL! THAT WAS GREAT! when she finally stumbles onto the right answer.

It could also be programmed to say, WHAT A FATHEAD YOU ARE, HAZEL! every time she misses, but the computer would not be to blame for that.

Once we load a program from tape into the computer we can change it around to suit ourselves. We can change the comments the computer makes — as, for example, by putting in Hazel's name to give it a personal touch. We can add ideas of our own, or take something out. If we prefer our own version of the program we can dump it on tape or a floppy disk and keep it. Once I found that a game program was beyond my computer's memory capacity. When I listed it I found an instruction which, when omitted, caused the game to run a bit more slowly but brought it within my range.

We are still talking about ready-made programs. What about the ones we can create for ourselves?

When we first start gaining hands-on experience at the keyboard we enter a wild world where the unexpected is constantly happening. We soon learn how much the computer can do with very little encouragement. Here is an innocent-looking little program:

```
10 A = A + 1
20 PRINT A
30 GOTO 10
40 STOP
```

But wait a minute! In the first place, how can A equal A plus 1? Anyone who knows any algebra knows that A equals A and cannot possibly equal more or less than itself.

It can in the computer world.

In computer language, the "equals" sign means something different from plain and simple "equals." It can mean "is equivalent to," which is only another way of saying "equals," but it can also mean "has the new value of."

When we write "A = A + 1" we are indicating that we want A to be increased by 1 every time the computer returns to the line it appears on, which is line 10.

Since we have given the computer no value for A, it automatically gives A the value "0," or zero. Zero plus one equals one. In line 10, then, when the program begins to run, A has the value of 1. The computer notes this fact and goes on to the next line, line 20.

Line 20 tells the computer to PRINT A. The computer prints 1.

Line 30 tells it to go to (GOTO) line 10. Back it goes.

Since A now equals 1, the computer finds that A equals A + 1 equals 1 + 1, or 2. It again moves to the next line, which is again line 20. Line 20 again tells the computer to PRINT A. It prints 2 on the screen directly under 1, and goes on to the next line, line 30, which sends it back again to line 10.

Since A now has the value of 2, A + 1 now equals 3. And so on. Thus, when we take the fatal step and run the program, what we get is a string of figures like this:

                              1
                              2
                              3
                              4
                              5
                              6 . . .

The line continues at high speed down the screen without pause and without missing a single integer, then scrolls off madly at the top as new figures appear at the bottom. As the numbers mount into the hundreds it becomes plain that the computer will continue to count off whole numbers in sequence, one below the other, until it wears out or the electric company runs out of power.

We have created a "loop," which means that the computer will go on printing numbers indefinitely unless we do something about it. It never gets to line 40, which tells it to STOP, because line 30 keeps sending it back to line 10.

Instead of sitting at the keyboard shouting, "Stop! *Stop!* stop!," we coolly press Control-C.

Pressing the Ctrl and C keys simultaneously causes this to happen:

                              755
                              756
                              757

```
758
∧C
! ERROR - CTRL-C STRUCK AT LINE 20
*_
```

The string of numbers has stopped. (Line 20 was being executed when Control-C was struck.) The prompt mark and cursor, ready and waiting, tell us we can now take over again. The best thing we can do is type LIST, so that the computer will print our program on the screen again, giving us a chance to look it over and make sure we understand why a loop was created from which the computer could not exit. There are several ways to correct the situation. Let's say we'd like the computer to print numbers from 1 to 20 but stop there. We rewrite line 10 to say:

10 A = A + 1:IF A > 20 GOTO 40

"If A is more than 20 then go to line 40 STOP." The computer now prints a column of figures 1 to 20, exits from the loop, and stops.

Though it demonstrates what a computer can do with very small programs, the above program is hardly a useful one. Incidentally, the original loop could have been a one-liner and worked just as endlessly:

10 A = A + 1:PRINT A:GOTO 10

The third instruction, GOTO 10, sends the computer back to the beginning of the line, thus creating the same endless loop. By separating instructions with a colon we can write several on one line.

But now let's do something useful. Suppose we want a multiplication table to appear on the screen. To save time and space we'll call up only the first three tables, up to 3 × 12, which

will give us everything from 1 × 1 to 3 × 12. We decide this ought
to do it:

```
10 FOR A = 1 TO 3
20 FOR B = 1 TO 12
30 PRINT A*B
40 NEXT B
50 NEXT A
60 STOP
```

Line 10: FOR A = 1 TO 3 means we want A to represent a
sequence of numbers from 1 to 3, one at a time. The FOR . . . NEXT
instruction is known as a *statement pair.*

Line 20: FOR B = 1 TO 12 means that we want B to represent a
sequence of numbers from 1 to 12, one at a time.

Line 30: PRINT A*B means that we want A to be multiplied by
B every time the computer comes to this line. The first time it will,
of course, multiply the first A (1) by the first B (1) and print the
result — 1.

Line 40: NEXT B means that we want the first A to be
multiplied by all the rest of the B's.

Line 50: NEXT A means, "Go through the same sequence with
all the other A's (2 and 3), multiplying them by all the B's."

Line 60: STOP means that when all these multiplications have
been accomplished the program is to stop.

When we run this program, we get what we asked for. We
always get what we ask for from the computer, but what we ask for
may not be what we had in mind.

In this case, we get a string of numbers, one under the other, all
the way from 1 (1 × 1) to 36 (3 × 12), with the earlier numbers
scrolling off at the top as the later numbers come on at the bottom
(our screen can display only twenty-four lines at a time).

We have our multiplication table, all right, but not in a very useful form. We wanted it in nice lines *across* the screen, so that all the numbers would stay put and we could look at them all at once.

When a program does not run properly, or to our satisfaction, it is because we have not given the computer the exact instructions needed. So we set to work debugging the program. Looking at line 30 we now realize we left something out. We left out the symbol that tells the computer we want things printed on a line across the screen. To indicate this we use a semicolon (;).

30 PRINT A*B;

We now run the program again, and this time we get the numbers in a straight line across the screen — all the way across in two long lines. So now we remember something else we should add:

40 NEXT B: PRINT

Here the instruction PRINT means that we want only the first A's multiplications with all the B's to be printed on the first line, with the second A's on the next line and the third A's on the next.

And because of one of the computer's peculiarities we also add a new line, which we will come to in a moment. The trouble with a computer is that it starts each number in the same place, without regard to how many figures it consists of. Ask it to print 3, 24, 452, and 964758 in a column, and it will give you:

3
24
452
964758

This is hardly the way we would write them down if we wanted to add them up. This sort of thing does not bother a computer, which is doing its addition in binary numbers anyway, but it bothers us. Fortunately there is an easy way to straighten up our multiplication table and make it look right by putting a new line, 25, in between lines 20 and 30:

```
10 FOR A = 1 TO 3
20 FOR B = 1 TO 12
25 IF A*B<10 THEN PRINT " ";
30 PRINT A*B;
40 NEXT B: PRINT
50 NEXT A
60 STOP
```

As you will recall, < means "is less than." The empty space between quotation marks calls for just that—an empty space. We are saying, "If A times B is less than 10, put one space ahead of it before printing it." We also remember to add a semicolon at the end of the line so that the empty space will stay on the same line as the single-digit numbers it affects. This time we get:

```
1  2  3   4   5   6   7   8   9  10  11  12
2  4  6   8  10  12  14  16  18  20  22  24
3  6  9  12  15  18  21  24  27  30  33  36
```

—all lined up for easy reading.

This program, too, can be written in fewer lines. Notice that wherever numerals and letters are next to one another spaces are omitted. The reason for jamming instructions together when possible is that each space uses up one bit in memory. The more memory we save, the more room we have left for other programs. Besides, if later on we ask to have the program listed, the computer obligingly displays it with the omitted spaces all inserted. Here is a two-line version of the multiplication table program:

```
10 FOR A=1TO3:FOR B=1TO12:IF A*B<10THEN PRINT" ";
20 PRINT A*B;:NEXT B:PRINT:NEXT A:STOP
```

What about a still more useful program, such as one that will keep a record of a bank account? How about one that shows dates, withdrawals, deposits, balance, and keeps a running account of interest earned to date? It can be set up in three lines, only one of which involves actual programming:

```
10 PRINT TAB(20)"SAVINGS ACCOUNT"
20 PRINT "DATE","WITHDRAWAL","DEPOSIT","BALANCE","INTEREST"
30 X = .000136986:B = 9458:PRINT "7/1",,,B
```

In line 20 the commas indicate that columns are desired.

In line 30, X is the amount of interest $1 draws per day at 5 percent annually. It will be used later. B is the balance in the account at the time we enter it in the computer. The two extra commas between "7/1" and B indicate that two columns are to be skipped.

We make a $150 deposit on the fifth day of the month, a $500 withdrawal on the tenth, and a $765 deposit on the twenty-third. For those interested in the details of the program, see the box on the next page. Here is the readout we would get:

	SAVINGS ACCOUNT			
DATE	WITHDRAWAL	DEPOSIT	BALANCE	INTEREST
7/1			9458	
7/5		150	9608	5.18244
7/10	500		9108	11.7632
7/23		765	9873	27.9829

It is equally easy to set up a checkbook record, but so far I have not bothered. I make an average half-dozen deposits or withdrawals per month in my savings account but write checks almost every day. Who wants to run to the computer every time he writes a check?

```
10 PRINT TAB(20)"SAVINGS ACCOUNT"
20 PRINT "DATE","WITHDRAWAL","DEPOSIT","BALANCE","INTEREST"
30 X = .000136986:B = 9458:PRINT "7/1",,,B
40 D = 150: B1=B + D:I1=4*X*B:PRINT "7/5",,D,B1,I1
50 W = 500: B=B1−W:I=5*X*B1+I1:PRINT "7/10",W,,B,I
60 D = 765: B1=B + D:I1=13*X*B+I:PRINT "7/23",,D,B1,I1
1000 STOP
```

Line 10: TAB(20) indents 20 spaces.

Line 40: B1 is the new balance. It equals the old Balance plus Deposit. I1 is our first Interest entry: 4 days time daily interest rate per dollar (X) times the old balance, which is B. By alternating use of B and B1, I and I1, it is possible to keep the old value for one and give a new value to the other.

Line 50: Now B becomes the new balance, and equals B1, the old balance, minus Withdrawal. Interest to date equals 5 times daily interest (from July 5 to July 10) times the old balance *plus* the interest earned up to July 5.

Line 60: Interest to date now becomes 13 days times daily interest times old balance plus interest earned up to July 10.

Line 1000: Just to leave plenty of room for more entries.

And yet, I'm tempted. Why not continue to enter them in the checkbook as always but put a batch of them in the computer about once a week? Every time I forget a check I have written and have to enter it out of order later on, I am tempted. In the computer the missing check could be entered in its proper place and the balance would adjust automatically from that point forward. Mistakes I have sometimes made because I couldn't even read my own figures would be a thing of the past.

A computer can be a great help to daydreamers. Let's say you are looking through the real-estate ads, wishing you could buy your dream house. "Here's one that sounds good for $59,000. Now, let's see — if we could raise $10,000 and get a twenty-year mortgage for the rest at 11½ percent, I wonder what our monthly payment would be?" A declining interest program will tell you at once, and give you a monthly breakdown of principal and interest if you want it. In this case the monthly payment will be $522.55.

How much is your car costing you to drive in these difficult times? Assemble your figures on mileage, maintenance, repairs, taxes, garage, insurance, automobile club dues, and years of service, and a simple little program will tell you all sorts of interesting things. (For a readout on a seven-year-old car that has not been driven much, see the box on the next page.)

The same program can be used repeatedly for any car or for the purpose of making educated guesses about the expenses involved in someone else's big gas guzzler, or what your own expenses might be if you drove your car more, or less.

Records kept for income-tax purposes can really make child's play out of the annual filling out of forms, and many things are stored cn floppy disks now that I never seemed to get around to calculating for myself on paper. For instance, a three-year record of fuel-oil consumption for purposes of easy comparison. Did that

CAR EXPENSES

ORIGINAL COST	2641
TRADE-IN VALUE	(1200) ←—(The computer
COST OF GAS	1645 subtracts this fig-
MAINTENANCE	1078 ure from the total)
REPAIRS	356
TAXES	764
GARAGE	3024
INSURANCE	1190
AUTO CLUB	212
TOTAL COST	9710

COST PER YEAR	1387.14
COST PER MONTH	115.595
COST PER DAY	3.7978
COST PER MILE	.245932

A 350 MILE TRIP WILL COST $83.562
    COST OF GAS: 12.069

To give a realistic picture of what the car was costing at the time, I set the cost of gas per gallon at $1. Mileage was 24 mpg. The last part allows me to input a projected trip of any length and gives me the cost based on the cost-per-mile rate adjusted to 29 mpg, which is what the car gets on long runs.

extra insulation job last year actually bring about a substantial saving? The computer tells me I saved 10 percent over last year and 21 percent over the year before, which at prices now current means savings of $207 and $480 respectively. What with one thing and another I seem to know more about my own affairs now than I did before I had a computer.

All work and no play would make the computer a dull companion, though, so let's look at some of the ways a person can have fun with a computer, and I don't mean just by playing computer games.

7

▀▀

Playing with Programs

In some ways the computer is the ultimate plaything, the supertoy, with which thousands of games can be played. In many of these the user makes push-button responses, in others he may have to enter a few figures or a word or two. The game itself may be difficult, but the technique of play is usually undemanding.

It is fascinating, at times almost awesome, to see all the twists and turns and subtleties of a complicated game reproduced by a computer, and then discover it can give you a very good battle as your opponent. In programming some games the problems are as complex as those confronting a programmer involved in more serious tasks, such as working out the trajectory for an interplanetary space vehicle or the specifications for a new piece of machinery. And although the programmer does the brainwork it is the computer that does the sleight of hand, so that in some circumstances it is hard not to feel that it may be smarter than you are. One good way to get over this inferiority complex is to do some programming yourself. Once you have written a program that makes the computer perform satisfactorily, you *know* who's boss.

By way of starting small, I wrote my own program for rolling dice. Only twenty-eight lines long, it includes everything that can happen in a dice game. It lets one player keep the dice as long as he wins, gives them to the other player when the first one loses, keeps track of each player's wins, and allows play to continue for as long as the players wish. Mine is for two players only, since I was not primarily interested in playing the game, and certainly not interested in developing a computerized gambling parlor.

The readout on the next page shows what the action is like. A random number comes up for each of the dice and the total is displayed, with the three numbers appearing on the screen one at a time in sequence. One player's loss is tallied as a win for the other player. Once the two players' names have been entered, a message appears telling the first player it is his or her roll, and the computer waits for that player to press the Return key. From then on the players simply press the key for each new roll.

In dice, a first roll of 7 or 11 wins; 2, 3, or 12 loses. When any other number is rolled first, that number becomes the "point" that must be made. If a 6 is thrown, then another 6 must be thrown for a win, and 7 now becomes the losing number; if a 7 is thrown before the point is repeated, the player loses.

One ready-made program I have enjoyed using in my own way is "Biorhythm," which will plot your biorhythms for any period of time you wish. According to the theory of biorhythms we are influenced from birth to death by three internal cycles, each with a different wavelength: physical, twenty-three days; emotional, twenty-eight days; and intellectual, thirty-three days. These cycles begin on the day of one's birth. Plotted on a graph, they are shown this way (see page 69).

FIRST PLAYER? MABEL
SECOND PLAYER? GEORGE
IT'S MABEL'S ROLL
6 2 8
6 4 10
5 4 9
3 2 5
4 3 7
YOU LOSE!
GEORGE'S TOTAL WINS: 1
IT'S GEORGE'S ROLL
6 6 12
BOXCARS! YOU LOSE!
MABEL'S TOTAL WINS: 1
IT'S MABEL'S ROLL
4 3 7
LUCKY SEVEN! YOU WIN!
MABEL'S TOTAL WINS: 2
IT'S MABEL'S ROLL
1 3 4
4 5 9
6 2 8
2 2 4
MADE YOUR POINT! YOU
WIN!
MABEL'S TOTAL WINS: 3

IT'S MABEL'S ROLL
6 4 10
3 1 4
1 2 3
. . . 15 more rolls involving
every point except 7 . . .
6 2 8
4 6 10
MADE YOUR POINT! YOU
WIN!
MABEL'S TOTAL WINS: 4
IT'S MABEL'S ROLL
1 3 4
5 6 11
5 5 10
2 5 7
YOU LOSE!
GEORGE'S TOTAL WINS: 2
IT'S GEORGE'S ROLL
1 1 2
SNAKE EYES! YOU LOSE!
MABEL'S TOTAL WINS: 6
IT'S MABEL'S ROLL . . .

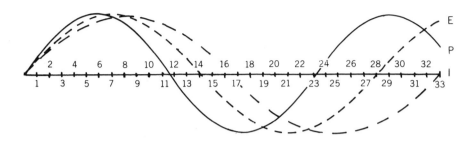

The horizontal line is called a *reference line*. When a cycle crosses this line, we are neither up nor down. Our physical, emotional, or intellectual condition is unstable; we are having a "critical day." Critical days occur twice per cycle. Here are the standard explanations of biorhythm cycles as they appear on the video screen:

PHYSICAL CYCLE (P)
UP: ENDURANCE AND STRENGTH AT HEIGHT.
CRITICAL: CAUTION - ACCIDENT PRONE.
DOWN: REST, REDUCE ACTIVITIES.

EMOTIONAL CYCLE (E)
UP: HARMONIOUS DAYS. ENJOY SOCIAL RELATIONSHIPS.
CRITICAL: CAUTION - UNSTABLE.
DOWN: STRESS DAYS, MOODINESS AND NEGATIVE OUTLOOK.

INTELLECTUAL CYCLE (I)
UP: CREATIVE DAYS, JUDGMENT AND PERCEPTION AT THEIR BEST.
CRITICAL: CAUTION - ERROR PRONE.
DOWN: BELOW PAR, AVOID DECISIONS AND NEW PROJECTS.

My personal interest in biorhythm data is limited, but I soon began to see in it a fascinating tool for historical research. For example, what sort of shape was Napoleon in at the battle of

Waterloo? How was Washington doing when he crossed the Delaware? What about Lee at Gettysburg?

Something had to be done, of course, about this note in the instructions: "Program restrictions require the dates you enter into the program to be between March 1, 1900, and February 28, 2100." For all graphs, two dates were to be entered: the date of the subject's birth, and the day the graph was to start on. Napoleon was born on August 15, 1769, and the battle of Waterloo was fought on June 18, 1815. Well, then, why not move the dates ahead two centuries to 1969 and 2015? Same difference. Well, not quite. Only those even-hundred years that can be divided by four hundred are leap years; 2000 will be a leap year, but 1700, 1800, and 1900 were not. Dates adjusted to any day after February 28, 2000, would need to have one day deducted from them to compensate for the leap year. Waterloo would have to be read as June 17, 2015, to make things come out right. But other than that everything worked perfectly and was accurate.

Napoleon at Waterloo, I learned, was in pretty good condition intellectually but a touch below par physically and emotionally. "Rest, and reduce your activities," a biorhythm consultant might well have advised him, "and watch out for moodiness and negative outlook." Two days after Waterloo Napoleon had a double critical day in the P and E departments, making him accident-prone and unstable, which must have been all he needed at a time like that.

Oddly enough, though, the victorious Duke of Wellington's graph makes it clear he should not even have got out of bed that morning. He was down in all departments.

General Robert E. Lee's biorhythms were better, but he would have done well to put off Gettysburg for about three and a half months, by which time he had a week coming up that was tops in all three categories.

Washington crossing the Delaware, John Paul Jones winning

his great victory on the *Bon Homme Richard*, and Patrick Henry delivering his famous speech were all up emotionally but otherwise having an average day. Still hoping that Napoleon might deliver the goods one way or the other, I tried him on the scene of his most brilliant victory, the battle of Austerlitz. He was slightly up in P and E, but bottomed out intellectually! In my desperation for a dramatic breakthrough I even tried Custer at his Last Stand, but no graph could have been more noncommittal.

My final effort was General Dwight D. Eisenhower on D-Day in World War II. A printout of his graph as it appeared on the screen follows. Because of its scrolling action the computer prints biorhythm graphs with the reference line vertical, but turning the page sideways will give the desired effect. If biorhythm proves anything, it may prove that generals have less to do with the way battles turn out than they would like us to believe.

```
                              DOWN                    UP
FRI   3   JUNE        P    E I            !
SAT   4              P E I                !
SUN   5               XP                  !
MON   6              X       P            !  ←——D-Day,
TUE   7              X            P       !  June 6, 1944
WED   8               I E               P !
THUR  9               I E                 X
FRI   10               I   E              !  P
SAT   11                I     E           !        P
```

I have adjusted the graph to show June 6 as it would have been in 1944. The X's in the graph are used to show points where two or more cycles cross, or the points at which they cross the reference line. General Eisenhower had a physical critical day three days after D-Day.

The best fun to be had with a computer, however, comes from setting yourself a problem and then figuring out on your own how to solve it. That bank account program, for example, started me daydreaming. What if it were my savings account and I had a brother-in-law who loved to come over and play games on the computer? (I don't have, but I dreamed up one named Carl for the purposes of the problem.) Now, I didn't mind Carl's playing chess and backgammon and blackjack with the computer, but I knew he was nosy, and the day might come when I was not around and he might decide to investigate some of my other floppy disks. I didn't want him to run a readout of my savings account because if he knew I had $9873 in the bank he'd try to borrow some of it.

Of course, I could simply hide the disk or keep it under lock and key, but that would be a nuisance when I wanted to use it. So why not add these lines to the beginning of the program:

```
5 INPUT A
7 IF A<>346 THEN GOTO 1000
```

Now if Carl tried to run the program this is what he would get:

?_

If he entered anything other than "346" the computer would simply print:

STOP AT LINE 1000

Just to tantalize the snoop, should he ever try to fool around, I went back and rewrote line 5 to make it read:

5 INPUT "CODE NUMBER?";A

Here "CODE NUMBER?" is a string literal, and A represents the figure to be entered. When the program is run, line 5 produces this:

CODE NUMBER? _

So far, so good. The only trouble was, I had noticed lately that Carl was beginning to glance at the instruction manuals and otherwise show interest in the computer itself. What if he learned that the command LIST caused the actual program lines to be listed? Then he could see the original balance as plain as day, and could figure out my current wealth to the penny. Very well, then, I would disguise that original amount! With fiendish ingenuity I worked out a new line 30 that looked like this (see page 62 for original program):

30 B1=ASC("$")/\3*1.2+89.8:B=NOT B1:X=.000136986

That ought to hold him! ASC refers to the "American Standard Code for Information Exchange," a code set used by the computer and generally referred to as ASCII. The /\3 following it means the number is to be cubed. So what I am asking for is this: the ASCII code number for the dollar sign, which is 36, to be cubed; the cube to be multiplied by 1.2; and 89.8 to be added, giving a grand total of 56077. The B=NOT B1 is an operation involving Boolean values. The NOT function complements the bits of the binary representation of 56077 and gives the result in decimal — 9458, the original balance. Now Carl would *never* be able to figure out what that balance was! I typed in the new line, listed the whole program for an overall look — and felt silly.

I had forgotten that the first two lines of the program would also be listed:

5 INPUT "CODE NUMBER?";A
7 IF A<>346 THEN GOTO 1000

There was the code number for anyone to see. All Carl had to do, once he had listed the program and realized what those first two lines mean, was to type RUN, enter 346, and watch my savings account unroll before his eyes.

Presently, the solution that everybody else has probably thought of by now occurred to me, and I rewrote line 5 and erased line 7. The program now began this way:

```
5 INPUT "CODE NUMBER?";B
10 PRINT TAB(20)"SAVINGS ACCOUNT"
20 PRINT "DATE","WITHDRAWAL","DEPOSIT","BALANCE","INTEREST"
30 X=.000136986
40 PRINT "7/1",,,B
```

Now any number could be entered and the program would run, but only I knew the number — my original balance, 9458 — without which no one could work out my current balance, not even Carl.

And of course now it became fun to think big. Why not raise my original balance to half a million and see how things would shape up:

DATE	WITHDRAWAL	DEPOSIT	BALANCE	INTEREST
7/1			500000	
7/5		150	500150	273.971
7/10	500		499650	616.538
7/23		765	500415	1506.32

Look at the way that interest grows! However, nobody should keep that kind of money in an ordinary day-of-deposit-day-of-withdrawal 5 percent interest account. Now, supposing I invested half of it in . . . Daydreaming again!

We have talked about the computer at work and the computer at play, but what about the important question, is a home computer a practical investment for the average family today?

No. Before it becomes indispensable the home computer will have to be less expensive, much easier to use, and have economical access to large data banks and special-services sources (these are already available, but are still too expensive for most of us). Home computers will also have to be more dependable. To quote the *New York Times* again: "As with any new product of technology, the first generation of personal computers has its share of lemons. According to the owners, manufacturers' and computer shops' service departments are good with technical problems, but design mistakes have crept up in several makers' early production models."

Computers are fine for hobbyists who can build and service their own, but for those of us who simply want to use them, they sometimes fall short. The instruction manuals are good at telling us what to do when everything is working properly, but do a poor job, if any, of explaining what may be wrong when everything is not working properly. The better manufacturers make a constant effort to increase dependability and notify users of possible improvements, but there is still much to be desired.

And yet, despite the limitations and frustrations, having lived with a home computer for over a year and used it every day it wasn't back in the shop, I would now feel lost without it. My personal affairs have never been in better order. Here are some of the programs I have written that I use frequently, most of them at least weekly, some of them daily:

Data for tax reports
    Contributions
    Utilities
    Business expenses
    Household expenses
    Trips
    Stock sales
    State and local taxes
    Dividends
Daily calendar of all appointments

Household inventory

Stock report

Car data

Heating-fuel consumption records

Safe-deposit box contents

Bibliography of computer literature

Basic terms of book contracts, individually retrievable

Number of copies of each book on hand (in which box in which closet; hardback, paperback, foreign editions, and so on)

Locations of all the odds and ends I used to spend too much time hunting for at least once a year, each item's location individually retrievable

To sum up, then: as of now, a home computer is really not worth having — unless you happen to have one.

There is one big exception to this rule, however: a home computer can be well worth having if there are children in the home.

8

A Family Computer

A professional toy designer named Larry Alcoff used his home computer to test a word game he had designed. He found it helpful, but according to a *New York Times* article he was ready to take a back seat to the younger generation.

> "My kids are much better with the computer than I am," he said, echoing other personal computer users. Mr. Alcoff's son Peter, 15, prepares for history tests by answering questions he's programmed into the computer. Another son, Alexander, 12, writes his own programs with a fluent knowledge of BASIC.
>
> "They can program better than I ever will," said their father. "They aren't awed by the computer. To them it's like learning to speak a foreign language."

His final statement may sound odd, but it makes sense. Young people who have lived abroad know that they were able to pick up the language and talk to everyone in sight while their parents were still trying to sort out the verb forms. Similarly, they find themselves at home in the computer world and get along better with computers than do most older persons.

The first day I walked into a computer store the manager told me, "We have twelve-year-olds coming in here who know more about computers than we do." But boys and girls don't have to be that old to make good use of computers. Even at ages five or six they can sit at a keyboard and enjoy learning the alphabet. If there are older brothers or sisters in the family, so much the better; they can think up and write the programs. Here is what one such older sister named Jessica did for her younger sister Amy:

"I decided to work out an alphabet program for Amy that would have the computer pick out a letter at random and show it on the screen," she told me. "Then Amy would have to find the letter on the keyboard and press the key that would match the letter on the screen. If they matched, I'd fix it so the computer popped off a row of stars. If she made a mistake, I'd have it run off some exclamation points — after all, she can't read yet, so I couldn't have it say a word, like 'Wrong!' — and then repeat the letter for another try."

A little program such as this was duck soup for Jessica. After a while, when Amy got so good at the first program she began to be bored by it, Jessica wrote a new alphabet program that worked this way (the underlined portions are the letters the user types in):

ABC?
? <u>D</u>
****

ABCD?
? <u>E</u>
****

ABCDE?

```
? G
!!!!!!!!!
? F
********
```

A B C D E F?

Almost before Jessica knew it, Amy was reading and knew lots of words, so it was time for some simple word-game programs. Jessica came up with one that asked Amy to make animals' names out of a group of letters:

ACT	TAR	NILO	ARBE	FLOW
GRIET	OSMEU	RHESO	MACLE	SNOIB

These would be displayed one at a time. There would be "Right!" or "Wrong, try again!" responses to each answer, and a scorecard of Rights and Wrongs displayed at the finish. And incidentally, the computer has another good feature. While it is never impatient, neither is it permissive. There is only one answer it will accept and that is a totally correct answer. If a child who was eager to make a good score were to look at "GRIET" and sort it out into "TIGRE," some fond parents might say, "Well, that's the way tiger is spelled in French, Spanish, and Italian, so I guess we should give you at least half-credit for that one, shouldn't we, darling?" The computer is made of sterner stuff. Unless you're using a French, Spanish, or Italian computer, you had better come up with "TIGER" or your score is zero.

For arithmetic, of course, the computer is superb. A problem such as "264 × 83 = ?" may need doing with pencil and paper, but once an answer has been worked out it is more fun to enter it in the computer and get an instant right or wrong reaction than to look up the answer in the back of a book. And when such a program is running there is no way users can make the computer do the figuring for them; they must work out the answers for themselves.

As students reach the stage of quizzes and tests the computers can be used in endless ways. Programs of questions and answers are helpful as drills, but they have another valuable function: the very business of entering a question-and-answer pair, then testing to be sure it runs properly, is likely to fix it firmly into the user's memory as well as the computer's. Once such a program has been properly designed, each set of questions and answers can be stored for later review and a new set substituted, and each new set can in turn be stored, so that before a final exam the whole lot can be used as a refresher course.

Multiple-choice questions, because of the amount of typing involved, are tedious to enter for limited personal use, but could be used by an entire class in schools where terminals are available — which brings us to an interesting side of computers, their time-sharing abilities. If a school has a dozen video terminals and one computer, all the terminals can be used at once, either for running a program, writing a new one, or any other normal purpose. The computer works so fast it can handle commands and instructions from many terminals at the same time, keep everything neatly separated, and still be waiting around for something to do.

Various programming techniques can make a quiz more interesting. For example, let's take a multiple-choice question:

    Q. THE INVENTOR OF THE GAME OF BASEBALL WAS:
        A. BENJAMIN FRANKLIN
        B. ALEXANDER CARTWRIGHT
        C. BABE RUTH
        D. ABNER DOUBLEDAY
    ANSWER? __

If the user answers with the correct letter, then RIGHT! TEN

POINTS FOR YOU! might appear on the screen. If not, then this might appear:

WRONG! THE CORRECT ANSWER IS:

Followed by a dramatic pause . . . and then the answer. Dramatic pauses are often fun to put in. In this case, the computer would be given these instructions:

PRINT "WRONG! THE CORRECT ANSWER IS: ";PAUSE(1000);X

where PAUSE(1000) stands for a pause of 2 × 1000 milliseconds, or 2 seconds, and X stands for the correct answer. This provides the suspenseful two-second pause before the answer appears. If the instruction PAUSE is given without the time instruction (1000), then the answer will not appear until the Return key is struck, whereupon this will be displayed:

WRONG! THE CORRECT ANSWER IS: B. ALEXANDER CARTWRIGHT

No, not D for Doubleday. It seems that Cartwright, not Doubleday, was the actual inventor of baseball.

Speaking of baseball, the computer can be a great help in keeping track of batting averages, pitching records, team standings, and other such statistics. Every record concerning a school or Little League team can be entered in a computer and updated after every game.

Where school grades are concerned, especially at high-school and college levels, the computer can provide an excellent early-warning system. Suppose a course involves frequent recitations, two or three quizzes each week, a weekly test, and a final exam. Grades in each category can be entered and weighted according to relative importance, and a final grade for the course projected on the basis of performance to date. The sense of false security an occasional good mark can bring is less of a threat when the hard facts are constantly visible.

For collectors, bird-watchers, junior financiers studying the stock market, astronomers, and naturalists, to give but a few examples, the computer is a perfect keeper of records, since the records stay in one place, remain readable, and are more orderly than they otherwise would probably be. And finally, of course, as a source of sophisticated entertainment the computer has only just begun its career, with human minds — mostly young ones — rapidly extending its potentials. Imagination, good judgment, the use of logic, mathematical skills, fast reactions, self-control — all these capabilities receive meaningful testing in some of the more complicated computer games.

It is a good thing a younger generation is coming along that understands and is not awed by computers, because for our own protection we need a general public that understands them. The more Americans there are who can think intelligently about computers, the better our chances of protecting ourselves from computer misuse.

A growing amount of information about each of us is being stored in data banks, making invasion of our privacy ever easier. An informed public would insist on safeguards against unauthorized access to this information. Even under the best of circumstances adequate safeguards will be difficult to maintain; without a general awareness of the need, life in America could soon become life in a goldfish bowl.

All great inventions have had the potential for both good and evil, whether automobiles, airplanes, X rays, dynamite, nuclear energy, or computers. Most of the gathering of information about individuals is honestly considered by the gatherers to be for the public good, and no doubt will be if the information is properly used and protected. But there are ways in which computers are being abused that are already costing us dearly and will do so at a rapidly escalating rate if we fail to develop better safeguards and security. As long as computers remain a mystery to all but a select few, computer crime will continue to be one of our fastest-growing industries.

9

Computer
Crime and Abuse

According to Donn B. Parker, an authority on the subject, legal experts object to the term "computer crime" on the grounds that it takes an expert to decide what is a crime and what is not. So Parker came up with the term "computer abuse," which is able to cover a multitude of sins — and crimes.

The *New York Times* reported on the case of a student who was a computer operator at a college's data-processing center and whose name "seemed to be synonymous with excellent grades during his years at" the college.

Three years after the student graduated the local district attorney charged that his good grades had come too easily for him, not to mention the grades of some other students at the school.

He was accused of "having changed 131 grades, of which 13 were his own, in the computer records of 15 students. He was charged with falsifying business records, bribe-taking, receiving a reward for official misconduct, and violating a state education law with respect to examinations. He could receive up to seven years in prison if convicted."

His own doctored grades had won him a Phi Beta Kappa key

and a place on the dean's honor list. For others, prices ranged from three hundred dollars from one student for falsifying twenty-two grades to about one hundred dollars from another for eleven changes, along with some free-of-charge upgradings for friends and relatives. Three years had passed before a physics instructor happened to notice a discrepancy between his own old-fashioned handwritten records and a printout of grades in the physics department.

Wherever records are kept by computer the temptation to alter them may be present. Without adequate safeguards such things as credit ratings, employment records, welfare records, medical, legal, and financial records are all vulnerable.

For that matter, now that they no longer need be huge affairs, computers themselves have been stolen, sometimes by students. The smaller and more portable they become the more tempting they are to thieves, and great numbers of computers are now used in all schools, from universities and colleges to high schools and elementary schools.

One student stole a terminal and took it home, eager to tie it in by telephone to the central computer. What he didn't know was that the terminal was equipped with an automatic answering device that identified it as the missing computer. His first call, quickly traced, brought the police to his door.

Some computers have been stolen, others have been attacked. An operator who worked nights in a dangerous section of town carried a gun. One night he became so infuriated at the computer's lack of cooperation that he pulled his gun on it and shot it right in the CPU. After extensive repairs it returned to the lineup without a gunslinger at the keyboard. But anyone who has struggled with a balky computer can understand what brought on the attack.

One-way shoot-outs have occurred on at least three continents. In Johannesburg, South Africa, a man thought to be a disgruntled taxpayer fired four bullets through a window at a computer used by the income-tax bureau. In Olympia, Washington, a man shot a computer in the State Unemployment Office. In both cases the computers' cabinets were merely dented. They went right on working while their attackers went off to jail. In Australia, however, antiwar demonstrators using a double-barreled shotgun made a total loss of a U.S. computer.

Most vandalizing has been done in other ways, and for a variety of reasons. Sometimes an employee has wanted to "get back at the company." At other times the computer's terrible, impersonal efficiency simply got on someone's nerves. One man short-circuited the computer's memory by shoving a car key into the works at a vital point. Others have used screwdrivers or other sharp-pointed instruments to inflict damage that on occasion has amounted to over half a million dollars' worth.

Demonstrators have often caused heavy losses. In Rome a few years ago three masked women held professors and their assistants at gunpoint at a university computer center while a male confederate poured gasoline on the computer and set it afire, causing over two million dollars' damage. Ten attacks on computer centers occurred in Italy during a two-year period. The group or groups responsible never made known their reasons for their attacks.

Even more serious was the 1970 bombing of the Army Mathematics Research Center at the University of Wisconsin in which one employee was killed and three persons injured. Besides doing $2.5 million of damage the blast destroyed computer data collected over a twenty-year period at an estimated cost of $16 million.

Destruction of software is often more costly and devastating than destruction of hardware. The computer records of a large insurance company were so voluminous that they required a tape librarian to keep them in order and produce needed tapes on demand. Her work, however, left her with enough free time to have love affairs with two of the men in the data-processing division. These involvements caused so much trouble that she was finally given thirty days' notice. For those thirty days she remained in charge of the tape library, with plenty of time to think of ways to get even with the company.

By erasing tapes or mislabeling them or filing them in the wrong places she managed to confuse the records beyond hope of recovery. The company had a duplicate set of all the tapes, but they were in the same building and also available to the librarian, who gave them the same treatment as the originals. Estimated cost of putting all the lost data back into the computer from scratch: $10 million. The damage was not discovered until after the librarian had left, and she was never prosecuted, simply because she was not a multimillionaire and could hardly make restitution. Today most banks and corporations not only have duplicates of all tapes but keep the two sets in widely separated places.

The persons responsible for these acts of violence and vandalism have not stood to gain anything other than the satisfaction of damaging a device that, for one reason or another, they have come to hate and fear, or the satisfaction of taking revenge on a hated employer or of attacking the Establishment. Although the monetary losses caused by such vandalism may seem high they are minor compared to the losses involved in the misuse, rather than abuse, of the computer for fraudulent purposes. The computer thief is definitely the newest big shot in the world of crime.

The trouble with computers is that many middle-aged people feel they are beyond comprehension, or not worth making the effort to understand, and most of the men and women in the top and middle management ranks of big banks and corporations are middle-aged or older.

When I talked to the data-processing center's manager about the new computerized devices they had set up for the use of the bank's customers he told me, "Young people take to them easily and like them, but older people are often uncomfortable with them." The same is true of most banks' top officers. They haven't the patience (or sometimes the ability) to learn much about how computers work. To illustrate the problem in another way I might mention a distinguished professor of mathematics who recently attended a course in computer programming with his two young sons. The boys caught on quickly; the professor's struggles to grasp the fundamentals of the computer caused great merriment in the family circle. Eventually, to be sure, he got the idea, and in the long run he surpassed the younger generation, but it took him longer to get going.

Banks and corporations, then, tend to look upon computers as a helpful new tool that can be run by bright young men who can be hired for good but not unreasonable salaries. And since computers don't make mistakes, what is there to worry about?

Plenty.

Robert Farr begins a book called *The Electronic Criminals* by asking, "What financial experience could the following people possibly have shared during the early summer of 1974?"

He then lists Liza Minnelli, Andy Williams, Walter Matthau, David Cassidy, and Jack Benny, along with a former chairman of General Electric, the chairman and president of Western Electric, the chairman of an important bank, a director of a large company, and two Washington lawyers. Beside each name are sums ranging from $108,000 to $538,000 — Andy Williams's loss.

The answer to the question is that they were all victims of the same swindle, and lost the sums mentioned. In this case the computer was not the principal tool of the crime. The swindle was an oil-drilling scheme in which the first investors, including some celebrities, quickly began to receive juicy returns on their investments because the "company" was supposedly hitting it big in the oil fields. This made it easy to attract other prominent people with money to invest, especially when they received reams of impressive computer printouts full of technical details about what was happening at each oil-well site.

As one of the victims, a banker, said later, "All I have for my money is about fifty pounds of computer printouts supposedly describing the operations." How could the computer make mistakes? It hadn't. It had simply been programmed to produce an extremely detailed accounting that was almost entirely bogus.

The mere word "computer" often seems to be enough to cause some people to lose their sense of judgment. A woman who had paid for several purchases by check at a shopping center certainly lost hers when a man stopped her on the way to her car and said, "Pardon me, madam, we've had a negative report on your bank check card from the computer."

He told her to give him her bank card and checkbook and — to show good faith — enough cash to cover the check she had written at Woolworth's, and said he "thought he could clear up the matter for her." She was to wait in her car till he returned.

The man said all this in front of a friend of the woman's and several other persons, which so flustered her that she obeyed him — anything to make him stop embarrassing her in front of all those people!

Half an hour later she was still waiting. By then it had dawned on her that the man was probably a crook who had watched her write several checks in various stores and then stepped up with his con game. She finally hurried to a phone to report the incident to the bank — but not fast enough. Purchases totaling $170 had already been made with her checks.

These are only two examples, one large and one small, of the many ways in which The Computer has been used merely to impress the victims.

In another type of fraud, bank computers become the innocent accomplices of crooks who never go near them.

My checking-account deposit slips have a code number printed on them in magnetic ink. This number, composed of funny-looking figures down in the left-hand corner of the slip, identifies my account in the computer. At some banks the customers' desk has blank deposit slips available for customers who have forgotten to bring along one of their own.

Now, suppose my bank was one of those (it isn't, I'm glad to say), and suppose I took a supply of the blank deposit slips, had my number printed on them in magnetic ink just the way it appears on my own slips, and then returned to the bank and slipped them into the supply of blank deposit slips at the customers' desk? How many customers, used to the queer string of numbers on their regular slips, would think anything about the ones down in the corner of the blank slips? If they thought anything about it they would probably conclude that the numbers identified the branch of the bank.

The deposits other bank customers made with those slips, however, would be credited to my account instead of theirs, and very soon I would be able to draw a lot of other people's money out of my account and quietly leave town.

Now, I hasten to add that I have never tried this scheme, but many others have and have gotten away with it, at least for a while. As customers begin to find money missing from their accounts an investigation gets under way — but often when the culprit is caught he has already spent the money. Prosecution in such cases has been erratic. Some banks prosecute the offender, others don't bother.

In 1966 a twenty-one-year-old programmer broke new ground: he was the first person to go on trial for a computer-assisted bank robbery, and he did not even work at the bank!

His firm was operating the new computer while the bank was training its own staff. When the bank turned him down on a loan he badly needed, the programmer took it out anyway — out of the computer. He did this by inserting a "patch" in the program that involved his own bank account. Normally a patch is a few new lines temporarily inserted into a program for the purpose of correcting a faulty operation. In this case the patch was an instruction to the computer to ignore any overdrafts he might make.

His original intention was to remove the patch within three days, by which time he expected to be able to cover the overdraft. But somehow three days stretched into three months and the patch was still there and by then he owed still more. At this point luck ran out on him, because the computer broke down and the bank went back to old-fashioned accounting methods while it was being repaired. His crime was discovered and he was tried and convicted, but was given a suspended sentence because of his youth and his lack of a criminal record.

He was, of course, fired by his company — but as soon as his trial was out of the way he was quietly rehired, and to do this his old company had to compete with offers from several other companies that had read about him in the newspapers. Good programmers were hard to find.

In this case the culprit had taken very little money and probably meant it when he said he had intended to return it as soon as he could. Other cases have been quite different in every respect, from the standpoint of both the crook and the bank.

In England a young bank director whom we shall call Smithers was only too happy to join the other directors in voting to computerize their accounting procedures. Once the system was in operation, Smithers managed to have instructions entered into the computer that diverted a steady stream of checks into the accounts of dummy companies he had set up.

To do this, he had a keypunch clerk enter the fraudulent instructions for him, and work overtime to do it! When the clerk got fed up and turned him in, Smithers calmly admitted everything, counting on the fact that his fellow bank directors would be unwilling to face the bad publicity, which would cause the bank's customers to lose faith in the bank and might also cause the companies that insured the bank's accounts to raise their rates. Not only that, Smithers had the nerve to demand a letter of recommendation to use in finding a new job!

He got the letter, and got the job. Another company hired him as its executive director. For the next three and a half years he used his know-how to milk that company's computer of about $100,000 a year.

When he was finally exposed he used the same tactics as before and with the same results — another letter of recommendation to still another company. But then when he had the arrogance to demand several thousand dollars' severance pay as well, he went too far. The company took him to court — but not on criminal charges. They charged him in a civil suit with breach of contract.

By law all bank losses are supposed to be reported. But rather than face bad publicity many banks have chosen to commit a felony themselves. When banks are held up by armed robbers they have no choice but to let the world know about it; computer crime is another story.

In armed bank robberies, according to the FBI, an average of about $10,000 is stolen. Nobody knows what the average is for computer bank frauds and embezzlements, but one estimate is $430,000 — forty-three times as much ill-gotten gain and no need to resort to violence.

Bank robbers who use guns are given stiff sentences when caught. But when computer criminals are brought to trial most judges know nothing about the workings of computers and have little to go by in deciding what should be done. To date most computer criminals have received light sentences or have been acquitted on grounds of insufficient evidence.

Although not a bank robber, one man actually · operated a successful stock swindle from his bedside telephone. He issued instructions to a computer, directing it to switch other people's stocks to his own account, then ordered it to erase all evidence of the transactions. When investigators finally got on his trail he fled before he could be arrested and is now believed to be living the good life under an assumed name on an island in the sunny Caribbean.

Some thieves steal because they are compulsive gamblers and need money to support their gambling habits. Such a person was the chief teller of a New York bank, a forty-one-year-old man with a wife and children and a modest home in the suburbs. He was paid $11,000 a year by the bank, but he received one important fringe benefit — he had access to one of the computer terminals.

At first he took money from only a few large, inactive accounts, mostly ones containing more than $100,000 that was left in the bank to earn interest. The chances of discovery were small and even then he could always trace the mistake to a "computer error" and juggle money around from other accounts to correct it.

When the auditors arrived on their regularly scheduled visits he had no trouble satisfying them and pulling the wool over their eyes since they really had no effective way as yet of auditing a computer's records. He even managed to make sure that the proper interest was posted on every account he had dipped into. The interest on one kind of account was payable quarterly on the last day of the quarter. Payment on another kind was due two days later. By shuttling money back and forth between the two kinds of accounts he was able to keep them all seemingly straight.

The chief teller continued to embezzle funds for three years to the tune of $1.4 million and still had not been suspected because nobody else knew the $1.4 million was missing. At first he had concentrated on only a few large accounts but as his need to gamble grew he tapped smaller ones, and his efforts to keep everything straight became ragged. He made notations on scraps of paper about his most recent withdrawals of other people's funds and stuffed the scraps into his pockets, which were eventually full of them — a far cry from the orderly bookkeeping methods expected of bank tellers.

By the time his embezzling was finally exposed he was betting as much as $30,000 a day and, like all compulsive gamblers, losing. But even then it was through no suspicions on the part of the bank officers or any good work on the part of the auditors that he was finally tripped up. He was unmasked quite by accident when the police raided the offices of bookmakers with whom the teller had placed tens of thousands of dollars' worth of bets on the horses. All patrons of the bookie joint whose names were found on slips were checked out by the police, and the police were understandably surprised to find that a man with an $11,000 salary was betting as much as $30,000 a day, and $3,000 on a single race. Further investigations soon led to his downfall.

His need for gambling money and his resentment of a bank that he felt had paid him poorly and used him badly were principally responsible for turning a man with no prior criminal record into an embezzler. Stealing from the bank did not bother him but toward the end as he was dipping into smaller accounts he was scrupulous in worrying about individual investors. Knowing that some of them were senior citizens who had put their life savings into the bank he was careful never to take more than $20,000 from such accounts, that being the amount insured in each account by the Federal Deposit Insurance Corporation. When this limit went up to $40,000 he went up to $40,000 too.

Because he showed proper remorse at his trial — whether he felt it is anybody's guess — he received only a twenty-month sentence, which time off for good behavior reduced to fifteen months in prison. While there, one thing he did was teach his fellow convicts a course in high-school math — including the use of computer video terminals.

Any machine that will give you nice green cash money when you stick a plastic card in it is bound to put the gleam of larceny in a lot of people's eyes.

One big problem with cash-dispensing machines is that of effectively identifying the user. Plastic cards, with identification data on their magnetic strips, are not a perfect answer, to say the least. Many other methods have been and are being experimented with — the length of one's fingers, for example. Two people with five fingers of exactly the same length finger for finger are hard if not impossible to find. Checking fingerprints with a laser light source is another possibility. But many law-abiding people object to the police-state idea of having their fingerprints on file and of thrusting their fingers into a place where all kinds of other people have had theirs. As Donn Parker says, "I am not going to put my hand on that same surface where a person who just finished eating a peanut butter and jelly sandwich placed his." He adds that a Japanese research team "concluded that lip prints could be more easily recognized automatically than fingerprints" — but who wants to kiss an IBM terminal?

My favorite of the ideas advanced so far is that of a Canadian inventor who would use the shape of people's skulls for purposes of identification. This would involve putting your head inside a sort of helmet that, if you were trying to impersonate someone else's head, would clamp down and hold you fast. (Can't you hear the muffled cries, and see the arms and legs flailing around?) A more acceptable idea is that of using brain-wave identification, but until this, too, does not involve sticking one's head into some sort of container, it seems unlikely that this idea will get off the drawing board, either.

The most sensational crime connected with bank cash-dispensing machines, however, did not involve a mere rip-off on an individual machine. It took place in Tokyo, where a man carefully planned a way to use cash-dispensing machines for a kidnapping payoff.

First, using an assumed name, S. Kobayashi, he opened an account in a bank that had 348 of the machines scattered all over Japan. By making withdrawals from a number of the machines and then calling the bank after each withdrawal to check his account, he found there was a gap of fifteen to twenty minutes between the time he made a withdrawal and the time the bank's records showed which machine he had used. This seemed to offer much safer possibilities than the dangerous business of having to meet someone in a certain known location in order to collect the ransom.

As soon as he had kidnapped the baby of a well-known Japanese movie and TV actor he phoned a demand for the ransom money to be paid into the account of S. Kobayashi by noon the next day. All he had to do then, he figured, was wait awhile and then withdraw the money from one of the 348 machines, with twenty minutes' time in which to make his getaway. He made a smart choice of machines, too, choosing one in Tokyo's largest railway station, where crowds were always enormous and hundreds of people used the machine every day.

Although his plan was ingenious, it failed because he did not know enough about computers. He did not know that the bank's computer could be quickly reprogrammed in a way that would tell the authorities instantly which machine S. Kobayashi had used. The police were there to grab him with his S. Kobayashi money card in one hand and the ransom money in the other. The baby was returned unharmed to its parents.

Not all computer crimes have involved the direct theft of money. Some have concerned unauthorized printouts of voter lists — very valuable to politicians — the theft of one company's computer programs by another, or unauthorized use of such things as credit data. In all these cases, of course, someone was making money out of the theft. And lots of real money has been involved in tampering with IRS income-tax records or in programming a computer to send Social Security or welfare payments to persons not entitled to them.

None of these misdeeds were invented with the computer, of course. In essence they all go back to the days of quill pens and ledgers. The process has simply become speedier and easier. Behind most computer crime or computer abuse lies the fact, well known to the criminals and abusers, that too few people know anything about computers to make computer crime a matter of general, public concern. Perhaps when a new generation has come along, one that has grown up with computers, has learned a lot about them, and is not awed by them, we will develop a society that can protect itself against computer crime far more effectively than is the case today.

10

The Computerized Home

Most predictions concerning the "World of Tomorrow" are comfortably vague about how soon Tomorrow will be with us. Sometime in the next century is the usual indication. But in the case of the computer's World of Tomorrow we are talking in terms of the next decades, perhaps no more than ten years from now. The following describes what one family's home may be like by that time — or sooner.

Ted and Helen Wallace have three children, Chris, fourteen, Linda, eleven, and Matt, nine. They are prosperous but not rich. Their computerized home is rapidly becoming the new way of life for many Americans.

The familiar alarm-clock tone interrupted Chris Wallace's dream in which two skillfully drawn figures were having a superhuman boxing match. He sat up in bed and said, "Okay, stop."

The alarm stopped. If anyone other than Chris or a member of his family had ordered the computer to stop the alarm it would have ignored the order. It was programmed to respond to their voices only.

Across the room the window shade rolled up, revealing a sunny spring morning. The lawn sprinklers had not been turned on because there had been a heavy shower during the early morning hours.

"Is Linda awake?" Chris asked.

YES appeared on the wall screen.

"Is Matt awake?"

YES.

"Intercom to Linda and Matt. Hey, you two! I finished my cartoon last night. Want to see it?"

Both came running to his room to see the cartoon.

"Okay, run Boxing," he ordered. Two figures he had drawn with a light pen in garish colors — not quite as skillfully as the ones in his dream — appeared on the screen. They wore boxing gloves and boxer's trunks.

"I'll take Blue Trunks," said Matt.

"I'll take Red," said Linda. They knew the Boxing animation program Chris had gotten for his birthday was keyed for random choice, so there was no way to tell which boxer would win. You drew your own figures and the program animated them.

Red and Blue swung wildly at each other, and once in a while the picture went haywire for a second or two, but finally Red Trunks knocked down Blue Trunks and won.

"What do you think?" asked Chris.

"It needs work," said Linda.

"Well, I know what's wrong. I'll put in a couple of patches to fix those places."

"Blue Trunks is a bum. I'm hungry," said Matt, and took his appetite to the kitchen. They could smell the coffee and hear the bacon sizzling in the skillet, because the computer had turned on the coffee maker and the burner under the bacon at the same instant their parents' alarm had sounded. The coffee had been turned off when ready, but kept hot, and the bacon would not be allowed to burn.

Out in the kitchen Ted Wallace had poured himself a cup of coffee and settled in a chair at the kitchen table to check the morning news. Video terminals cost so little now that there was one in almost every room in the house, and each could be used independently of the others. This prevented all those squabbles they had had in the early days, when there had been only one terminal for all to use.

Ted was reading his personalized "newspaper." He had programmed the computer to bring him a brief digest of the important news stories. If he wanted to read more about one of them he asked for the full story. Since his sports interest was baseball the computer gave him all the news about last night's games, the standings in both major leagues, and switched to full video for taped highlights of the Red Sox–Yankees game. If he wondered about some player's batting average or a pitcher's statistics he could interrupt, get the information he wanted, and then return to the programmed material.

Next he read Art Buchwald's column, and then a column by his favorite political commentator. He had the editorials' titles listed and called up one that interested him. He had finished it and was looking over the index of feature stories when his wife joined him.

"Have you looked at the classified ads yet?"

"No, but I will."

The Wallaces were considering buying a secondhand catboat if they could find a good one. Ted went to the keyboard, typed in a specific listing — CLFD-CATBOAT — and two listings for second-hand catboats appeared, but neither appealed to them.

"End News," he ordered, and the screen went blank. A small charge would be credited to the news service of Central Data Processing and at the end of the month their total news usage cost for that month would automatically be drawn from their bank account and credited to the news service. The charge would appear on their monthly statement along with almost everything else they bought or used during that month. Cash, and even checks, were almost a thing of the past. Nearly all financial transactions were handled within the computer system. Most purchases and service charges went on their Compute-A-Credit account, which gave them thirty days to "pay" either the total amount or a part of it. If they paid only part of the amount the rest was carried at a very hefty annual interest rate, just like in the old days of credit cards. A nation of people used to credit was not willing suddenly to pay cash on the barrelhead for everything they bought, as the computer's automatic transfer system would have had them doing. Compute-A-Credit, however, was generally popular. The big advantage was that one no longer had to carry credit cards and worry about losing them or having them stolen.

Helen was thinking about a dinner party they were going to give the next evening. After breakfast she sat down at the keyboard and turned to her husband.

"How about doing a paella tomorrow night?"

"Sure they haven't had it here before?"

"I'll check." She called up a list of the dinner parties at which she had served paella and checked the guest lists. "No, I've never served it to any of tomorrow night's crowd."

"Olé!" said Ted. "Let's have it."

Helen asked the computer for her recipe for paella, adding that there would be ten for dinner. Her recipe appeared on the screen with all amounts adjusted for ten — so many chicken breasts, so much sausage, so many clams and shrimp, the proportionate amounts of saffron and rice, and so on.

Next she called up a succession of local supermarket ads to see if there were any bargains she wanted to take advantage of. She chose the supermarket she wanted to place her order with, then entered her grocery list and directed it to the store. When she went there later her order would be waiting for her.

"Now let's see if Norton's is having that men's shoe sale," said Helen. She checked the store's ad and found that the sale was on. She had been after Ted to get himself a new pair of loafers for a month or more. He wasn't much better about shopping by computer than he had been about going to the stores directly in the old days.

"Bring me that outline of your foot, Ted."

She queried Norton's shoe department about brown loafers, traced the outline on the screen with the light pen, and was told that a pair of Baxter loafers were available in his size. Ted nodded, and she placed the order. He stood up.

"Well, I'd better get to work. I'm off to the office."

"Have a good trip!"

"I will. Yesterday the traffic was terrible. I passed two of the kids on my way across the kitchen!"

Ted's office was a small room off the kitchen. Doing most of his work at home was still new enough to seem strange.

"You know, it still amazes me that nobody foresaw how the computer would help solve the fuel shortage." He glanced at Matt, who was busy with a second bowl of cereal — having decided the first one tasted good he had returned for an encore. "Matt, would you believe it — back in the days before you were born we used to drive as much as seventy thousand miles a year?"

Matt looked at him blankly.

"Where did you go?"

"Well, I spent about twenty-five thousand miles of it driving into the city to my office, there and back five days a week — alone. Now I go once a week, and take the train."

Everyone in Ted's firm still spent at least one day a week at the main office because, as he said, "You have to know the people you're working with, and that's one thing you can't do by computer."

The rest of the time he conducted his business by computer from his home. Because of the commuting time saved and the added efficiency of the computerized approach his work took far less of his time than it used to. Workdays generally were becoming shorter and shorter.

He looked over the previous day's reports, held videophone conferences with one or two of his associates, and checked by computer with his lawyers concerning a couple of legal points in a new contract. All the information he needed appeared on the screen, including the actual statutes involved. He made a printout of the material for further study.

The children had gone back to their rooms to do their schoolwork because today was a "home day" for all of them. Under the new system they went to school every other day, alternating days each school week. In this way the teacher's daily classes were split in half, increasing the opportunity for individual attention.

On home days students worked on computer lessons. Under the Asimov Method developed by the science writer Isaac Asimov they were given a good deal of time for their own special interests and could pursue those interests in creative ways.

Linda, for example, was becoming deeply interested in ornithology, the study of birds, and already knew far more about birds than anyone else in the family. Through the computer she could draw on all the material that existed in libraries all over the country. If she wanted information on evening grosbeaks she could call up articles, color slides, and even short moving pictures showing evening grosbeaks.

While Helen was still in the kitchen the doorbell rang. If the person at the door were one of their friends who had been keyed into their computer, the screen would have flashed that person's name. The doorbell button, when pushed, "read" the caller's fingerprint by means of laser light. In this case, however, the message that appeared was:

STRANGER - 5' 8" TALL, 154 LBS., DARK HAIR, MALE

"Intercom front door," ordered Helen, then said, "Who is it?"

From the speaker outside the front door a voice answered, "United Parcel."

"Oh, it's my dress!" Helen opened the door and accepted the package from the deliveryman.

When she had tried on her new dress the family assembled for a look.

"Very nice. It's just right for you," said her husband. She eyed herself in the mirror and shook her head a bit sadly as the children chimed in their agreement.

"Well, it doesn't look all that right to me, but I can't fight city hall, can I?" she sighed.

In the past Helen had been inclined to choose clothes that looked well on her except for the colors she sometimes favored. This was not because she had bad taste; it was because, like many people, she was partially color-blind. Now she subscribed to a Color-Match program that indicated the colors and shades and combinations that suited her hair, eyes, and skin tones. No individual person could have gotten away with dictating color choices for her, but the impersonal computer could.

The terminal buzzed to call attention to a message on the screen.

BILLINGS OPINION POLL:
DOES YOUR FAMILY FAVOR ALL-BEEF FRANKS OR ORDINARY WIENERS?
    ENTER "A" FOR ALL-BEEF.
    ENTER "O" FOR ORDINARY WIENERS.
    ENTER "U" FOR UNDECIDED.

Ted glared at the screen, then stepped to the keyboard and punched "X" several times, causing the query to disappear.

"This polling business is being done to death! What do we care about their crummy franks?" he growled. "That was nothing but an advertising ploy, a weighted poll for some outfit that's pushing all-beef franks. Talk about loaded questions — 'all-beef franks' versus 'ordinary wieners'! This sort of nuisance has got to stop!"

Ted belonged to a growing minority who refused to answer any of the incessant "instant polls" that were plaguing computer users. Too many people still meekly answered everything, however.

"I've got a question for you, Dad. We were talking about it at school," said Chris. "What do you think of the idea of voting by computer?"

"Put me down 'N' for 'Not Much.' The individual identification system isn't certain enough yet," said Ted. "Too many chances for fraudulent votes to be slipped in. Still, they're debugging the process, and there's no doubt about it, instant elections are coming. Almost instant, anyway. Even in a presidential election the computer will be able to project a winner about five minutes after the first states start voting. What a crazy world it's getting to be! Fool computer takes all the fun out of some things. No suspense!"

Chris sighed. "I knew you'd be old-fashioned about it."

Before his father could get a lecture started on the virtues of being old-fashioned the doorbell rang and MARTHA HARRIS flashed on the screen. Linda ran to the door and admitted two women who were part of Helen's supermarket car pool — they no longer drove to stores by themselves in separate cars. After the ladies had made flattering comments on her new dress she changed clothes and they left for the market.

The supermarket looked much the same as always — from the outside. Inside, aisles and shelves of merchandise took up much less room than they had in former years.

The same packages of breakfast food, salt, sugar, coffee, spices, cookies, flour, frozen foods, and everything else were on the shelves and in the freezers, but in smaller quantities. Stores were glad to accept computerized orders but knew they would lose a vital amount of business if "impulse buying" were eliminated. Often half the items a shopper finally bought were chosen simply because the shopper saw them and decided he or she wanted them. Consequently the delivery section was located at the back of the store, so that customers would have to walk down at least one aisle to reach it.

True to form, everyone pushed shopping carts around the store and picked out several additional items, either on impulse or because they had forgotten they needed them. They also chose their own meat, fish, and fresh vegetables, since they were not yet willing to leave those choices to the computer.

When they reached the delivery section their additional purchases were added to their orders and they were given a printout of the charges for each item and the total. The total charge was automatically transferred from the customer's bank account to the store's account — a holdover from the old, well-established system of paying cash for groceries.

At home Linda had spotted an unexpected bird on the bird feeder and had rushed to the computer to check it out. She thought it was an indigo bunting and she was right.

Matt was drawing a diagram of a section of computer circuitry, using a light pen on his screen. Though only nine, he was fascinated by the inner workings of computer hardware and was learning fast. He was the only member of the family who was deeply interested in that side of computers.

Chris was taking a break from his math lesson and was playing a complicated Space War game with a friend a couple of blocks down the street. The game went light-years beyond what the earliest versions of space games had had to offer. The boys had been waging a very sophisticated battle, off and on, for several days. After a while they suspended hostilities and stored their game, ready to be resumed at the exact point where they had left off. Before hitting the books again they got in touch with several neighborhood buddies and set up a ball game for three o'clock.

Chris's father was glad to hear it.

"I want all you kids to get some exercise, especially on a nice day like this. I'm going to play a round of golf later on myself, and your mother's going to play tennis."

Like many fathers he looked upon the computer as a mixed blessing. Between it and wall-screen television there was too much time spent staring at video screens! It was getting so some people hardly left their homes anymore.

When Helen returned from her shopping Ted was checking the stock market. He had also asked for the day's stories on computer crime, a subject he found both fascinating and disturbing. As better safeguards were developed and more people understood computers it had become harder to pull off the fast ones that had long been so common, but for every advance in security there was a computer criminal somewhere working on ways to beat the new development.

"Here's a dandy, Helen. Read this." He showed her a printout he had made of a news item about a jewelry store caper.

Using chronometers linked by computer, a man and his wife had each gone to a different jewelry store and bought diamond rings in the $50,000 range. Their bank account contained $55,000, enough to cover one of the purchases but not both. In both stores the clerks were accomplices in the attempted rip-off.

By tying the chronometers in to the store terminals on temporary lines they were able to have both sales reported at the same instant. The idea was that it took a few seconds for the purchase price to be transferred from the customer's account to the store's. An APPROVED signal would be sent back to the second store as well as the first — and the husband, a former bank computer programmer, knew that once an approval had been sent no further check would be made until the run-through of accounts after the stores had closed. The chances of two charges coming through at the same exact nanosecond were so remote that no safeguard covering the possibility had been built into the computer.

The only reason the scheme had not worked was that the timing had been *too* perfect. Hit by two signals with such incredible precision, the computer had balked and returned NONFUNCTION. One of the clerks had panicked, one thing had led to another, and all four of the crooks were in custody.

Before dinner the Wallaces had a video chat with Helen's great-aunt Mary, who was seventy-five and confined to a wheelchair. She had just finished her usual Tuesday afternoon of bridge via computer with three old friends, two of whom were also shut-ins. For invalids and shut-ins the home computer was an undeniable boon, one that made all sorts of activities possible again. For many it was both companion and nurse. It provided reading material if desired, or read to those who needed that help. It was always ready to play games, provide puzzles, or even, in a general way, to gossip by drawing on a fund of information about what was going on locally and nationally — material read into Central Data Processing daily, under careful supervision, by an organization of volunteers. It also monitored the shut-ins' health and reported to a central health agency, alerting the staff to anything that might justify a "house call" by computer from a physician on duty.

That night Ted took the whole family to a stage show in which people performed live. His theory was that life could become a mere shadow play if a video screen constantly stood between a person and three-dimensional reality. At home, when the family left, the security system was in full command. Subtle sensors were set to detect an intruder's presence, should he somehow manage to break into the house despite the protection that had been pro-grammed into the computer. Importantly, it was even ready to draw on auxiliary power in case of a brownout (a drop in voltage) or a total outage, both of which were becoming an ever more familiar hazard in the United States as well as in many other countries.

The Wallaces' security system had been adequate so far, but Ted never left the house without an uneasy feeling. How soon would some smart burglar find a way to breach the latest safe-guards?

In the computer's fast-approaching World of Tomorrow some

of the things described above will definitely happen, some may not, but all of them *can* happen. The computer, for both good and ill, will touch and transform every aspect of our daily lives.

Some scientists seriously believe that one day computers will surpass us in intelligence and render human beings superfluous. But unless we lose the ability to pull the plug on the computer, my bet remains on Man.

Glossary

Analog computer   A computer that makes comparisons, that is a "measuring stick" rather than a counter. Clocks with hands, gas gauges and speedometers with pointers are all simple forms of analog computers.

Arithmetic/logic unit (ALU)   The circuits in the CPU that work out arithmetic problems and make logical decisions and comparisons.

Assembly language   Instead of using binary numbers, as machine language does, assembly language represents those numbers with combinations of letters that are understandable and can be remembered (CMP, M, RLC, DAA, for example). It is more difficult to learn and use than a high-level language such as BASIC.

BASIC   An acronym for Beginner's All-Purpose Symbolic Instruction Code, one of the more easily understood high-level languages.

Binary digit   The binary digits, 1 and 0, are used to represent all numbers, letters, and symbols used by the computer.

Bit   An abbreviation of binary digits, each bit being either a 1 or a 0 (ON or OFF).

Bug   An error in a program or instructions (software) or a defect in the functioning of equipment (hardware). Faulty soldering on a memory board can cause the computer to lose memory, for example; proper soldering would *debug* the board.

Byte   Eight bits in a series.

Central processing unit (CPU)   The heart and nerve center of a computer. It contains the accumulators, the arithmetic/logic unit, and the control section, which takes care of timing and makes sure that the accumulated data, instructions, and other material appear in the proper sequence.

Chip   A square or rectangular wafer of silicon, usually measuring from 1/10 to 1/4 inch on a side, upon which several layers of an integrated circuit have been etched or imprinted, after which the circuit has been encapsulated in plastic. (See *Integrated circuit*.)

Circuit   The complete path of an electric current.

Computer   An electronic calculating device that is capable of storing, processing, and producing information.

Control   See *Central processing unit*.

CPU   See *Central processing unit*.

Data   Any information that is fed into the computer for processing.

Debug   See Bug.

Digital computer   A computer that processes information in response to signals, each of which is a separate "On" or "Off" (binary digit) signal.

Diode   An electronic device with two terminals that allows current to flow in one direction. See *LED*.

Firmware   Programs that reside permanently in read-only memory (ROM) whether the computer is powered up or shut down.

Floppy disk   A plastic disk with a magnetic surface upon which programs and data may be recorded in segments of concentric circles by a recording head similar to those used in tape recorders.

Hardware Memory and circuit boards, keyboards, LED displays, video terminals, floppy-disk machines, tape recorders, printers, and all other equipment, electronic or otherwise, involved in the operations of a computer.

High-level language A programming language that is easier to understand and use than assembly or machine languages. See *BASIC.*

Input Data and instructions entered into the computer by a user or programmer.

Instruction A word or symbol (PRINT, GOTO, STOP) that guides the operations of the computer.

Integrated circuit (IC) An electronic circuit that has been miniaturized and imprinted and etched on a silicon chip.

Internal memory A computer's own high-speed memory, as distinct from the memory of peripheral materials such as tapes and floppy disks on which data are stored.

K "Kilo," from the Greek, means "thousand." In computer language K stands for "kilobytes" and represents 1000 (more exactly, 2 multiplied by itself 10 times, or 1024) bytes.

Keyboard Several rows of keys, usually four, arranged somewhat like a typewriter's keyboard, and containing extra symbols and functions in the case of a video-terminal keyboard. The digital computer used for this book also has a small keyboard, more commonly called a *keypad,* made up of four rows of four buttons, which are used to put the computer into operation.

Kilobyte See *K.*

LED (light-emitting diodes) Electronic devices that display letters or numbers on a readout panel, such as the one on the face of the digital computer, where the symbols appear in red.

Light pen A device resembling a pen with which a user can draw lines on the video screen that become visible.

Line printer A high-speed printing machine that reproduces on paper each line that appears on the video screen. Printouts of programs and data can thus be made for additional safekeeping.

Loop One or more instructions that are executed repeatedly in sequence.

Machine language Binary-code language, which is the only language a computer "understands." All other languages must be converted into machine language before the computer can make use of them.

Memory Those circuits of a digital computer that store data and instructions.

Microprocessor A small integrated circuit containing a central processing unit.

Nibble Half a byte, or four bits. Also *nybble*.

Object program A program that has been converted from high-level or assembly language into a machine language the computer can understand. See *Source program*.

Output The data a computer transmits to a peripheral device such as a video terminal or line printer.

Patch A few lines temporarily inserted into a program for the purpose of correcting a faulty operation.

Peripheral device A piece of equipment attached to a computer but working outside it, such as a video terminal, floppy-disk machine, or printer.

Printer A peripheral device that provides printouts of computer data.

Program A list of instructions written in a specific sequence designed to produce certain results or information. When "the computer makes a mistake," this is where the mistake originates — as the result of an error made by a human programmer.

Programmer The designer and writer of programs.

RAM Random-access memory, in which information can be stored at locations that are directly accessible to the computer for almost instant retrieval. See *ROM*.

Read/write memory Memory stored on tapes or floppy disks or on integrated circuits within the computer that can be eliminated by erasure or have changes and additions written into it.

ROM (read-only memory) Memory in which permanent information is stored. This information cannot be written into, and remains in the computer even when the power is off.

Smart video terminal A terminal that has its own microprocessor (central processing unit).

Software Sometimes referred to as "documentation." Software includes anything written into the computer by a programmer or user.

Source program A program written in high-level or assembly language that the computer is able to translate or convert into an object program. See *Object program*.

Store To *store* information in a computer, on tape, or on a floppy disk means to save it in the computer's or the peripheral device's memory. *Memory* and *storage* are interchangeable terms.

String literal Any portion of a statement enclosed in quotation marks. In the statement PRINT "KEEP OFF THE GRASS", "KEEP OFF THE GRASS" is a string literal, so called because it is reproduced literally, exactly as given.

Video terminal Any terminal that involves a CRT (cathode ray tube) similar to those used in a television screen. Video terminals for programmable home computers include a keyboard.

Index